Crossing the Burn

God bless!

(signature)

Feb 2009

www.jyjones.com

Booklocker.com, Inc.
2003

Crossing the Burn

J.Y. Jones

DEDICATION

To the mountain people of Appalachia, who are my own flesh and blood, and to my mother, Mary Ruth Jones Higdon, whose lifelong dedication to me forms a backdrop for this book, as well as a template for one its main characters.

CHAPTER 1

Indian Park in 1956 was a quiet place, a mountain place, a slice of Appalachia where people were private but their affairs were mostly common knowledge. The town was situated in a small, flat valley amid ancient, rounded peaks, with an assortment of rooftops clustered wall-to-wall. Twin spires of the Baptist and Methodist churches stood in mute competition, prominent landmarks as one arrived via the pass from Cherokee City. A light rain fell, clouds hung low over the basin, and a piercing whistle from the afternoon freight train sounded shrill in the distance, then faded away into a prolonged and pervasive stillness.

Rough clattering from a flathead automobile engine once more shattered the dreary gray autumn silence. The vehicle was blocky and black, a vintage 1949 sedan from Ford Motor Company. It chugged up a rain-slickened hill toward a modest white house on the edge of town. The machine fell abruptly quiet after it rattled into an unimpressive yard and slid to a stop, its whitewalled tires painted dirty orange by sloppy mud from the rutted road. A cotton-topped boy hurried to a window in the house and flung back crisp white curtains, then wiped away condensation for a better view outside. The driver's side glass of the car was open, despite brisk cold and a drizzling rain, and a red-faced man could be seen behind the steering wheel. He was smiling broadly and waving, while moisture and cigarette smoke billowed from his mouth.

"Mama, it's H.K.!" shouted Travis Jackson. "He told me he'd come by next time he was going quail hunting!"

"Mm. Don't know about this," Ruth Jackson muttered as she hurriedly tidied up her living room. The worst disorder rearranged, she glanced at herself in a hall mirror as she headed for the door. She was a beautiful woman, with smooth skin the color of fresh cream, brown eyes that seemed to clash with her light complexion, and a slim, appealing figure. Her hair was a tangle of natural blonde curls that seldom needed much attention. Her face looked flushed and her tasteful makeup had worn thin in the course of a hard day's work at Indian Park Diaper Factory. Adjusting quickly, she joined her boy at the door.

"Howdy, Ma'am," said the visitor cordially in a coarse voice, removing his hat in greeting. He let his eyes linger only briefly on the pretty lady before turning to the youngster. "Travis, ye wan' go huntin', son?"

The boy looked at his mother with the look of a hungry puppy, big eyes pleading. The woman was already shaking her head instinctively.

"Can I, Mama? Can I?"

"'At boy sho' 'nuff needs t' go, Ma'am. We jes' might brang home a mess o' birds. How 'bout it?"

Ruth surveyed H.K. McCard warily, deliberately weighing her options. H.K. was lanky and balding, and sported a moderately big belly hanging over his belt. He always smelled of men's lotion, and kept his thick facial hair cleanly shaved. Today he wore a bright hunting cap, which rode on his head slightly askew. There were little blue veins visible in the temple area of his face, prominent enough that one couldn't help but notice them. His red nose was oversized, deeply scarred by skin problems, and sported a few squiggly surface blood vessels as well. He had a very slight droop of his upper eyelids, a condition that masked the upper half of his hazel eyes. Overall, H.K. wasn't much to look at, but appearances were of little concern to her boy, who loved this middle-aged hunter much like a father. Ruth sometimes let the youngster accompany H.K. on raccoon hunts and other outings, but usually only when there were other respected people along. H.K. had a notorious rowdy streak, and Ruth just naturally didn't trust him. Being a product of these mountain environs herself, she fancied herself a pretty good judge of local men.

Ruth's husband was, in fact, a son of this same part of northern Georgia. He was now a retired serviceman, but he had taken his whole family all over the country and half the world since World War II. After retirement from the army he had continued to work for the government, and he was on the road constantly when he wasn't overseas, where he happened to be at the moment. Masculine attention to her maturing son should have been most welcome, though quite often she found herself worrying. H.K. was reputed to be a little heavy on liquor, a habit for which she harbored strong disapproval. Today the man seemed steady on his feet and his speech was as tidy as a sermon. She glanced again at Travis's intense eyes, and found herself wavering.

"Maybe so, H.K. Done your homework yet, Travis?"

"Yes, Ma'am. All but a little. And I can do the rest when I get home."

"Back by dark, H.K.?"

"Won't be gone more'n two hours. Jes' wan' t' show Travis whur 'em quail is. An' how a bird dog like Petunia works th' stuffin' out'n 'em."

"Okay, I guess so. Son, you be careful. Please don't shoot H.K., or anybody else."

"Aw, Mama, you know I wouldn't do that," said the youth as he spun to leave the room. As he disappeared he added, "Thanks, Mama. Be right back, H.K."

In a dark corner of his bedroom closet stood Travis's spanking-new 12-gauge shotgun, which he quickly retrieved. Younger brother Bobby was playing a board game on the floor with his little sister, Sue, and they paid scant attention while their sibling pulled on his worn high-top clod busters. Travis bulged his jacket pockets with a dozen or so shotgun shells, then scampered back to the living room. He kissed his mother on one cheek and burst through the screen door into the chill and dampness. He slid his shotgun into the car's back seat, and then climbed aboard the

9

old Ford. Its heavy door slammed shut with a firm, metallic thump, and black exhaust smoke fumed as H.K. pushed the accelerator.

The car smelled of whiskey and tobacco and dogs and leather and gunpowder, but to Travis's young mind such fragrances conveyed rampant excitement. He had ridden in this same vehicle on quite a few 'coon hunts with H.K. The man had a 'coon dog for which he had paid $500 cash, and he was fond of describing how he had counted out twenty-five twenty-dollar bills for that purchase. Such a price seemed unimaginable for a mere canine, nearly enough to buy a car, but most locals acknowledged that H.K.'s dogs were good, really good. And oh, how those dogs could make some awesome music, baying up and down every creek and hollow in the mountains, while campfires roared, and boasting and bragging and tall tales lasted deep into the night. The boy felt a little shiver of excitement as he recollected. But on this day H.K.'s dogs would be English pointers, not Walkers or red bones or blue ticks.

"Where are your dogs, H.K.?" he asked over the engine's din.

"In th' trunk, same as always. 'Ese bird dogs don't make as much racket as 'coon dogs, son, e'en when 'ey's ridin'. Not usually, nohow. Stink jes' as bad, though."

"Yeah, I can smell them. Where are we going?"

"O'er t' ol' Sion Holman's place. Saw 'im in town yestiddy, an' 'e swears 'ey's two coveys jes' befo' ye git t' th' creek. If'n 'at's so, we'll be eatin' bird fer supper, boy."

The two companions bounced down the dirt road, easing along in places so as to avoid deeper furrows carved into the sticky red clay while still maintaining the vehicle upright and out of yawning side ditches. H.K. shifted deftly between gears as necessary, the floorboard stick transmission intimately familiar. Down the steep hill they plunged, past a drab tan house where Poss and Tot Wilson lived. Its joyless windows were without curtains, and a good number of glass panes were cracked or completely missing and replaced with cardboard. The tacky patchwork stared at the world through unchanging walls framed in fake brick tarpaper. Smoke curled skyward from a slightly tilted chimney, indicating that someone was home, but no light could be seen in the windows. Probably the power company had cut off their electricity again, Travis thought to himself. A sagging, rotting sofa spanned much of the front porch, and a potpourri of straght-backed wooden chairs were randomly scattered about. One crippled chair with a missing front leg still leaned idly against a big chinaberry tree just beside the porch, where it had been since the previous summer.

Ruth Jackson had been uncomfortable moving into a house in close proximity to such people, but when they had moved to Indian Park a year before, there had been no other rental property available. Her husband had wanted Ruth and their kids to be near his own family during his upcoming overseas tour.

Usually the boisterous Wilson men, old Poss and his two boys, were out sipping beer and spitting tobacco juice into their cluttered yard. They had a worrisome habit of casting a menacing eye toward any passerby, and sometimes making catty comments to whoever was in the road. Seeing no one at the house, Travis couldn't help but seize the opportunity to stare at the ramshackle dwelling as they idled past. His unruly neighbors had never really threatened him, even when he walked past their house, but there was still a sense of tension, and he was relieved that none of the Wilson bunch was in view.

"I don't see any Wilsons out today, H.K. Unusual. I guess all this wet and cold is keeping them inside."

"Reckin so, boy. Ain't much t' 'at bunch, nohow. 'Ceptin' ol' Tot, an' she's 'bout three ax han'les 'crost th' rear.

Travis chuckled a little. Tot did carry a little extra weight, in stark contrast to the rest of the family.

Smooth pavement lay dead ahead, and after crossing some rough railroad tracks there was considerable improvement in the ride. The hamlet of Indian Park was coming up, with its old buildings nestled into a cleft in the mountains on three sides, and a broad valley tapering away to the west. Neither man nor boy spoke as they passed the jumbled, disorderly complex of structures that was Wheeless Lumber Company on their left, and a now-defunct marble finishing plant on their right. Next came a whitewashed building that housed the Bank of Indian Park, a community landmark and main commercial center in town. The institution was situated on one edge of an old Cherokee Indian meeting ground and ball field, a place that was said to have been the only flat, open ground for miles around before arrival of the white man. Their course then carried them down Main Street through the center of the village. H.K. waved at several acquaintances as they passed, including Banker Barksdale, president, owner, and chief officer of the bank. As far as the boy knew, Banker was actually the man's name, because nobody ever referred to him by anything else.

They rolled past a big brick two-story building that was Tinley Furniture, run by Don Tinley. Don's son, Hooter, was Travis's best friend, and they did have some good times together. Travis's thoughts flashed immediately to a wooden boat he and Hooter were assembling in the Tinley basement. The craft was being created from massive boards and tongue-and-groove one by four lumber, held together with nails, glue, and sticky black tar. Many weekend hours had been invested in that boat, and still there was much work to do. Prospects of trying out their fabrication on the nearby Etowah River were never far from Travis's mind, and he and Hooter talked about their ideas constantly.

There were several grocery stores in town, as well as a drug store and barber shop. Graham Motor Company, a Ford dealership, was the flagship business of Indian Park, and its yard was freshly raked and its shrubbery was cut back neat and trim for the winter. A shiny new '57 Ford coupe sat in a showroom window, and two gleaming new pickup trucks were parked on thick, frost-browned grass out front. The local school, where Travis was an eighth grader, came into view next. There were only eight grades at Indian Park School, and after finishing there students moved up to high school at the county seat. Or else they dropped out altogether, an option that was exercised with too much regularity.

"Yo' mama sho' 'nuff watches out fer ye, boy. Ye'd thank I'm th' devil er somebody, th' way she tawks when we wan' t' go huntin'."

"Naw, it's not that, H.K. She just doesn't think I'm old enough. I guess she overlooks how many rabbits and squirrels I bring home. And this here shotgun has a heap more kick than my little old .22, so maybe she's scared of it."

"A kick it sho' 'nuff has, li'l buddy. 'At it does. Sho' 'nuff be right keerful wi' it. Be min'ful o' where ye's pointin' 'er an' she'll brang in th' groceries, though. Handy as a switch on a cow's tail, by golly."

Indeed the new shotgun was plenty powerful. And its double barrels were a new item for the boy. It was somewhat of a trick to master two different triggers, and he had discovered for himself that you don't put a finger on each at the same time when shooting. It's an index finger on one trigger to shoot, after which one moves that same finger to the other trigger for the next shot. Mistakenly putting an index finger on the front trigger and a middle finger on the back trigger had caused him considerable grief just a week ago. He had been crossing a footlog in a burned-over forest behind his home when a covey of quail had burst from a grassy ditch underneath the downed trunk. He had never even shot at one of the fleet birds, but this had seemed an ideal chance. Travis had swung his shotgun toward them, but instead of a succession of two shots he had inadvertently detonated both barrels at once, cleanly missing the birds and thumping his shoulder so hard that he had lost his balance and fallen backwards off the log.

He had landed miraculously intact but extremely shaken, and somehow he had missed numerous rocks and sharp spikes that filled the small ravine. He had laid for several minutes contemplatng a pointed stump between his left rib cage and his left arm, a natural daggar that was tapered and black and awful, a waiting skewer that could have easily pierced completely through his body. He had sustained a nasty scratch on his arm, and as they motored along he fell silent for a time, reaching under his arm to feel a hard, healing scab through his flannel shirt. He shuddered as he contemplated his close call once more.

That he was still alive seemed more than a chance occurrence. The boy was convinced that there had to be more to it than that. He shivered again as he reviewed that incident in his mind, and for several minutes he said nothing as he and H.K. traveled. He couldn't help but wonder how one explains such things to a hunting buddy. Would H.K. understand, or would he indeed want to? Travis decided not to mention it, since there was that aspect of the episode that revealed his own total inexperience, evoking fear he might be thought stupid. On the other hand there was a mystical aspect as well. Stupidity he was comfortable enough discussing, even his own—but supernatural—no way he could bring that up to H.K. Yet the boy couldn't deny that he had sensed some kind of unfamiliar personage nearby while he had lain there, a new and pleasant and comforting closeness to...what? Maybe it had been a guardian angel. Whatever it was, it had provided him protection, and that was all he knew for certain. And the whole affair seemed almost like a dream now, receding in memory like mist on a moonlit night. He had discussed it with no one, and had been afraid to mention the matter even to his mother.

"Yep, 'at's fer sho' a fine shotgun, aw-rite," said H.K., breaking into the boy's reflection. "Sears makes a good 'un, Daddy always said."

"Your daddy has a shotgun?"

"Well, naw, 'e ain't got no shotgun. 'E likes Sears rifles, I mean. "E bought 'at ol' Savage pump 'e's got fum Sears nigh onto a hunnert years ago. Ye know 'e ain't no shotgun man. Lawd, 'e gives me enough fits o'er mine. Shotguns an' bird dogs an' quail huntin' is fer sissies, t' heah 'im tell it. But in 'at regard, I ain't m' papa's son. I love seein' m' dogs point an' 'en brang 'em birds t' hand adder th' shootin'."

The shotgun was a gift from the boy's parents for his thirteenth birthday a few months back. He still loved his old .22 rifle, and he sure as heck wasn't going to let H.K.'s father, Hank McCard, know he was using a scattergun these days. Hank was the boy's squirrel-hunting buddy and another of his best friends, and like many mountain men he held strong opinions on almost everything. One of his favorite prejudices was the virtue of rifles and the absolute uselessness of shotguns. It was cowardly and even dumb to use anything but a rifle on squirrels, or on anything else, as far as Hank was concerned. If you couldn't use a rifle on it, it wasn't worth hunting. Hank would adamantly declare this with a frequency and a finality that left no other word to be spoken on the subject.

While they talked, H.K. reached inside his hunting coat, felt around tentatively, and shortly he deftly produced a brown paper sack, crumpled tightly around the neck of a concealed, flat bottle. Taking both his hands momentarily from the big steering wheel, he opened his bottle, laid a coal black cap on the worn leather seat between them, and guzzled a long swig. The burn of alcohol in his throat felt familiar and comforting, and as soon as the sensation subsided he took another long swallow. H.K. glanced over at his companion, who watched him intently. He shoved his bottle in Travis's direction without replacing the cap, and then on second thought retracted it.

"Got t' give 'er a try sometime, boy, but not whilstye's wi' me," he said with a wheeze. "Least not 'til ye got 'nother year er two b'hind ye. Mighty good wildcat stuff 'ere, grow hair on yo' chest faster'n a 'coon kin climb a tree. An' 'at can't be nothin' but good, I figger."

"No, thanks, H.K.," replied the boy after an awkward hesitation. He was glad his friend had already withdrawn his impromptu offer. His mother espoused that there was a dreadful wickedness to this thing called alcohol, an attitude cemented by her trials in coping with an alcoholic father and brother. There was no room for middle ground between

15

teetotalers and those who seemed enslaved to brew. The boy wa
conditioned to avoid a first-hand encounter with such a malicious liquid

On leaving the main section of Indian Park, they passed by sever
more residences before wet pavement once more gave way to mudd
country road. The worst sections had been shored up with coarse grave
but still it was slow going. The rain gradually subsided to a very fir
mist, and then stopped completely. By the time they reached a
overgrown, fallow field on the Holman place, the air held a hint o
clearing weather, though everywhere vegetation still dripped and ditch
yet ran with water.

"Hot-o-mighty! I wuz 'fraid we wuz gon' hafta sprout fins t' hunt,
said H.K. as they pushed open the Ford's creaky doors. "Looky at th
blue sky up 'ere!"

The car was halted in an acute curve next to Sion Holman's fiel
and H.K. took one additional deep swig from his bottle before they g
out. They opened the trunk, and two sparkling white pointer dogs spran
forth, brimming with pent-up enthusiasm. They shook themselves brisk
on hitting solid ground, took care of postponed business for a minute o
two, and then quickly disappeared into the weed-choked field. A ver
business-like metallic sound of loading shotguns punctuated the chill ai
and right away the man and boy ascended a muddy red embankme
adjacent the parked car.

"Hunt 'em, Petunia! Look close, Daisy!" yelled H.K. at interval
while the boy tried to imitate the man's encouragement to the dog
Those snappy pointers quartered back and forth, seeking their quarr
intently, appearing and disappearing at intervals, while the pair o
hunters followed with dedication. Every waterlogged hedgerow, ever
dripping plum thicket, every drenched patch of kudzu drew the dog
scrutiny, but all to no avail. The boy longed to see for the first time th
mysterious canine phenomenon known as "pointing," indicating that th
dogs had found their quarry, but it was not to be this day. Maybe s
much precipitation had kept the birds in hiding all day, or perhaps th

driving rain had simply scoured away all scent. For whatever reason, the field was sterile, except for an occasional meadowlark or towhee, which the dogs disregarded with dutiful disdain. Ever so often, H.K. stopped and reached for his liquor bottle, imbibing yet another gulp of whiskey before shouting at his busy dogs and moving on. The boy noticed that his friend's step had become a bit unsteady, but he tried to ignore it. His thoughts were much less of H.K.'s drinking than of a fervent desire to experience his first taste of a real, dog-assisted covey rise.

An hour of searching produced nothing at all, except for wet feet and a complete soaking of the boy's jeans all the way up to his knees, the inevitable result of dragging through interlacing, dripping vegetation. Finally, H.K. motioned blankly toward the car, and they began their retreat, accompanied by the dogs, whose eagerness seemed not in the least diminished. Still, light was just beginning to fail, and it was no doubt time to call it a day and come back some other time. By now H.K.'s speech was as thick as sorghum syrup, his eyes had lost their sparkle, and his facial muscles had relaxed so that he was almost devoid of expression.

"'Tain't like ol' Sion t' lead me wrong. Betcha 'em birds is here. We'll hit 'er again in a few days, boy," he mumbled indistinctly as they approached the car. "We won't let 'em whup us."

Travis broke open his shotgun, slipped both shells from the chambers, dropped them into his pocket, and then descended the steep bank first. Just before he took a final leap to the road, there was a loud cry from his friend, followed by a totally unexpected shotgun blast. H.K. almost knocked the boy's feet from under him as his slid into the miry ditch, groaning like a combat casualty. Blood gushed from a fist-sized wound on the right side of his chest, where innumerable pellets had ripped away his jacket and reached underlying flesh. H.K.'s shotgun stood impaled barrel first at the bottom of the red clay bank, and there was a gruesome trail of crimson smeared into the wet soil.

Horrified, Travis tossed aside his own gun and knelt beside his friend, who was conscious though badly wounded. H.K. groaned and writhed in the ditch, cursing with each breath at his ineptitude in losing his footing. The shotgun had fallen first on its butt, discharging its potent load, and then had cartwheeled away. How could things go so wrong? Perplexed bird dogs gathered around, as if trying to help, getting in the way and licking H.K. in the face even as blood spurted in a ghastly flood. Travis ripped open H.K.'s jacket, and there was sticky hemorrhage everywhere. While the man writhed and moaned, the boy wadded up his handkerchief and with shaking hands stuffed it into the torrential flow, only to see his pitiful cloth quickly inundated.

"Go git he'p, boy," coughed H.K. with difficulty. His eyes rolled back revealing white sclera, while blood trickled from one corner of his mouth. For a brief moment the man seemed to go limp and lose consciousness, and the terrified boy wondered if he was dead.

Travis looked around frantically, but there was no traffic on the remote road. Desperate, he tried to rouse his friend with cries and vigorous pats, while the terror of the situation nudged him towards outright hysteria. He could hear himself breathing a distraught prayer, half-saying the words, half-thinking them. He didn't know how he managed it, but as he worked to stop the massive bleeding he calmed down significantly. H.K. opened his eyes once more, sending a course of relief through the boy. He found himself telling his injured friend, in an oddly tranquil voice, that he was going to the Holman house for help. He thought he heard someone behind him, and as he stood up, he even looked around expectantly. There was no one visible, but he distinctly felt that he was not alone. He concluded that it was absolutely necessary to leave H.K. and go for help, so before he left he looked in the car and located an old cleaning rag, which he added to the packing he had already placed in the wound. H.K. once more appeared momentarily unconscious, but roused as the boy stood up once more to leave. Travis broke quickly into a run, sensing that time was against his friend, who continued to bleed at an alarming rate.

"Take th' car, son," the wounded man called weakly, his failing voice clearly pleading.

The boy ignored his advice, knowing full well that a straight shift transmission was far beyond his driving abilities. He had practiced some in his yard at home with the '55 Mercury his mother drove, but its automatic transmission was entirely different from the clutch-shrouded mystery of H.K.'s car. His own legs would have to run for help.

Down a steep, muddy hill he went, skidding with each step but covering a mile to the Holman house in minutes that seemed like hours. He developed a sharp stitch in his right side as he pushed himself along, but he shut his mind off to incidental pain and kept on running as hard as he could. The road led through ominous rushing waters at Sharp Mountain Creek, which was high, unbridged, and threatening. The raging current appeared uncrossable as he approached.

"Oh, God," he cried out loud. "Help me!"

A confidence surged within him as he splashed through unscathed, using whatever rocks protruded, and continued his critical dash for help. The Holman home was disappointingly quiet as he entered the yard, and repeated yells as he approached went unheeded. He banged briskly on the door, hoping, praying. Nobody was home.

His uncertainty began rising once more, and he thought of breaking in and using their phone. He wasn't sure they had one, however, so he quickly chose the only other alternative—there was another house a half-mile down the road. His hands ached from pummeling the unyielding wood of the Holman's front door, but his breath had caught up some, and he felt a new surge of vigor course through his frail frame. He took off once more as a gray twilight descended, running as hard as he could run, pushing his body past its limit, and refusing to feel tired. Soon a colorless, unpainted house loomed ahead, and like a racer sprinting for the finish line he used every ounce of his strength to reach its low, sagging porch. There was a beaten old Studebaker parked out front, missing its back windshield and one headlight. Gone also was the front bumper, the driver side door was bent inward, and one rear fender was slightly crumpled.

Travis knocked loudly again, wincing with pain and yelling and making as much noise as possible while praying aloud that someone would be home. To his great relief, two inquisitive young men opened the door. In bated breath he attempted to explain H.K.'s plight. They yelled something to another person inside the house, and pointed the boy toward their delapidated car. An older woman appeared at the door as they prepared to depart.

"Git in, kid. 'Is Studebaker's faster'n it looks. It wuz doin' o'er a hunnert miles a hour las' weekend comin' back fum Florida. It'll git 'is guy t' th' hospital quicker'n quicksand. Cherokee City's closest. Maw, call th' sheriff an' tell 'im we'll be blowin' through like a stock car racer!"

In seconds, it seemed, they had slipped and slid up the road, blasted through the angry waters of Sharp Mountain Creek like a speedboat, and were back at the parked Ford. H.K. had managed to erect himself since Travis had hurried away, and there was a trail of blood from the ditch leading around the back of the car to the driver's door, as well as a broad smear of crimson on the window glass. He was now sprawled prone on the ground, still conscious but lacking enough energy to rise. He rolled slightly while trying to raise his head, and smiled weakly as the Studebaker skated to a stop.

"I be dog if'n 'e didn' find somebody. Mighty glad t' see ye, boys," H.K. said hoarsely. He managed to make it onto his side as the trio jumped out, and with difficulty he wheezed, "Whynja take th' car, Travis?"

"I can't drive a straight shift, H.K.," the boy explained meekly as the rescuers lifted and tugged to get the injured man into their back seat. The two were most considerate and were apparently oblivious to copious blood and mud being daubed into their vehicle.

"I'll take 'im t' th' hospital, an' ye take th' kid home," said one of them, obviously the oldest. The second boy nodded in agreement, and with a growl of its engine and a spinning of muddy tires the Studebaker was gone. Travis gathered up both discarded shotguns, loaded a pair of terribly confused bird dogs back into the trunk, and then indicated to his benefactor that everything was ready.

"Whur ye live, kid?"

"Indian Park. I'll show you," said Travis, a slight tremble in his voice, as the youth started the Ford and expertly manipulated the gear shift. Shortly they were retracing the route back home, while the boy's heart rate subsided and hope for his friend revived. H.K. had ceased to bleed actively and had looked like he just might make it. But all that blood certainly made it seem mighty bad, and he couldn't be sure.

"Yo' gut-shot friend's drunker'n a boiled owl, ain't 'e, boy?"

"He drank some. Probably too much," said Travis. He paused before adding, "Actually, way too much. And he's not shot in the guts, it's his chest."

"'At hard-drinkin' likker'll git a man in trouble e'er time, Maw sez," replied the driver, ignoring Travis' anatomy lesson. "We's Holiness an' we ain't much on cussin' an' hard likker. 'Ceptin' 'round New Y'ars and the Fo'th o' July."

The car of Sheriff Hoke Hatfield was parked in the boy's yard when they arrived. Ruth Jackson rushed headlong outside and embraced Travis as he descended from the vehicle, pulling him to herself warmly. After a prolonged embrace under the porch light, and a few tears from both of them, she pushed him back and looked at him eye-to-eye.

"Did you shoot H.K., son?"

"Me? Heck, no, Mama. He fell down and shot himself."

A distinct measure of relief covered Ruth's face, and she turned the sheriff.

"There you have it, Hoke. Shot himself. And they say he's going be okay?"

"The deputy who escorted them says he's got some damage, a he's in surgery, but he'll survive. Glad your boy's not at fault. Goo work in getting help, Travis. I'll take H.K's shotgun, if you don't min I'll get your driver back home, and I'll make sure somebody picks H.K.'s car."

While cleaning his own shotgun that night, the boy pondered. H was normally a light sleeper, and this would doubtless be a difficu night. His mother had already talked to H.K.'s wife by phone, and th boy had by now been reassured that his friend's life was out of dange There was much comfort in that realization.

The alcohol issue resurfaced in his mind as he contemplated, and s did that treacherous muddy bank. Then he considered the droppe shotgun and a seemingly random blast that could have gone in an direction. He relived repeatedly his desperate and reckless dash for hel He shuddered as he considered far worse possibilities that had n occurred.

And that sensation he had felt so strongly—was that the sam Presence he had felt when he fell off that log? It had seemed so real, s close at hand, and apparently very powerful—and so supportive and caring. And H.K. could very likely owe his life to it.

But what was it? And was there any way H.K. could be aware of i The youngster honestly didn't know, but he would visit his injured frien at the hospital tomorrow night. And he planned to ask him.

CHAPTER 2

"So ye wuz some kind o' hero las' week, huh, skinny boy?" sneered Mutt Mayberry, one of the older boys attending eighth grade at Indian Park School. "Shoot a guy 'n 'en go fer he'p andye's a hero, I guess, squirt."

The derisive, mocking tone of voice couldn't be mistaken. Mutt smelled of week-old sweat and wood smoke, and his medium-length dark hair was slicked back tight, oily-style, and was almost dripping with tonic. He had small, deep-set eyes sitting underneath thick eyebrows that were wrinkled into a constant frown. His full sideburns came down on his face almost to each corner of the jaw, pushing perilously close to the maximum length allowed by the school's principal. A pack of cigarettes protruded from his shirt pocket, and a comb handle peeked out of a back pocket of his baggy pants. Mutt had joined the army for a brief stint a year before, and had been stationed in Panama when he got into some kind of trouble and got busted. Rumor was that he had been given a dishonorable discharge, and returning to school had been a most unwelcome option for him. He was here more to avoid a sweat-soaking sawmill job than for any disposition towards learning.

Travis Jackson gulped a bit, then stammered only a little in his reply. He was accustomed to bigger boys, since his class consisted of a sizable proportion of holdbacks, most of whom had failed grades. Others had quit school, acquired a dose of job reality, and returned to try and get educated. So many of the boys had to shave before coming to school that students of normal grade age unavoidably felt stunted or grossly underdeveloped.

"Nobody said I was a hero, Mutt. But when H.K. shot himself, I did what anybody else would've done. I went for help. And you don't have to ask me who shot H.K., ask him. He's out of the hospital, and he was down on Main Street yesterday."

"I ain't studdin' 'bout 'im, nohow. I ain't studdin' 'bout nothin'. already know all I need t' know. An' 'at goes fer 'ese dufus teachers 'ere too."

"Then why don't you just quit again, Mutt? You don't like it here and you don't make very good grades, anyway, do you?"

"Who ye t' be criticizin' m' grades? I'll stay 'ere long as I like When I'm ready t' move on, I will. An' not befo'," he muttered. He gave the smaller boy a firm but benign shove as he turned and walked away down the hall. "Gonna git me a smoke befo' recess is o'er. Smarty-pant kid."

Indian Park School was housed in one of that era's common mixed up buildings that meshed old-style architecture with a more modern addition. A main one-story portion had been constructed in the 1920s using conventional soaring, multi-paned windows and a steep peaked roof. A more recent addition had two stories, considerably lower ceiling height, and a pancake flat top. The two sections were connected by open covered walkways. A medium-sized auditorium of older architecture stood between these structures, and down a hill and a steep flight of stairs behind was the gymnasium. Worn playground equipment could be seen on the end where the youngest children attended classes, and the smoking tree was at the opposite extreme. Seventh and eighth graders were allowed to stand under or near this tree for outside smokes, but lighting up was not permitted inside buildings or anywhere else on school grounds.

Travis just shook his head as his adversary walked away with a swaggering gait. He followed Mutt with his eyes as he disappeared toward the smoke tree, and then walked back toward his classroom. where a math lesson was coming up. His attention quickly returned to more important matters immediately at hand. Teachers in the institution were excellent, dedicated professionals of the old school, dispensing basic education and firm discipline, and from Travis they demanded a high level of performance. Most of them were able to maintain strict order among the unteachables while still continuing to challenge those who wanted to learn. When required, the iron hand of principal Eli Thompson could be counted on to mete out justice swiftly and consistently. Older boys feared and obeyed the stout, wiry principal as dutifully as anyone else, because he was plenty man enough to command their respect.

Thompson was even-handed in matters of authority, but he was not hesitant to pick a favorite student to do special tasks in and around school. Such a person was Travis Jackson, in whom the principal saw great potential. He met the boy in the hallway and greeted him with a cordial hello as they passed. Travis entered his classroom, where Miss Leila Tillman was putting a series of math problems on the blackboard. He took his seat and began to arrange his notebook for class.

Desks were arranged in rows from front to back, and teachers assigned seats based in great part on who was most likely to cause trouble. The most problematic students tended to be in front, with more studious kids toward the back. The teacher's desk was impeccable, reflecting her meticulous style, and on it were several reference books, in addition to the usual textbooks. A big, black copy of the Holy Bible lay on one corner, used mainly when the teacher read from it for daily devotional just before first period started. Over the chalkboard hung a large picture of George Washington, wearing his never-changing faint smile. Travis couldn't help but think of Mona Lisa with a white wig every time he looked at that portrait. Flags of the United States and the State of Georgia were displayed prominently, one in each front corner of the room.

The large, green chalkboard was the most modern in eye relief visual aids, and several problems Miss Tillman had carefully scribed there appeared challenging and complex at first glance. Travis looked them over, and was relieved to see that most of them on closer inspection were fairly familiar.

The bell hadn't rung yet, so most students were still outside. In back of the room were two older kids, Trixie Wills and her boyfriend Red Roper, talking in low and serious tones. Trixie was completely grown though only fifteen years old, and possessed the filled-out body of an adult woman. Her mere presence caused hormones to rage in all the boys. Trixie and Red engaged in fervent, barely-hidden kissing on bus rides to and from basketball games, providing plentiful fodder for gossip in school, tantalizing tales that often spilled over into the streets of Indian Park. Travis couldn't help but fantasize about such goings-on, sometimes to a point of great distraction. He stole an inquisitive glance at the pair before taking his seat and starting to copy down problems from the board.

Shortly the bell sounded, and a rush of eighth grade students crowded into the classroom. Among the first through the door was his impish friend, Hooter Tinley, who was small in stature and had a generously freckled face that didn't seem to match his dark hair and eyes. Hooter was bright enough to be a top student, but his academic interests were regrettably shallow. He always seemed bored with classroom subjects, and his main attention focused on some kind of mischief. He held his own with bigger boys in the class by virtue of sheer wit, and most of them were reluctant to engage him in any altercation, verbal or otherwise. Sometimes his replies to any attempt at intimidation would leave bigger, slower boys scratching their heads, wondering if they had been maligned or complimented. As far as Travis was concerned, Hooter's most irritating habit was calling him "Curly-top," a reference to Travis's ample blonde hair, but fortunately the nickname was seldom mentioned when more susceptible subjects of ridicule were around. Bubba Bean, the class fall guy, came in behind Hooter, accompanied by his cousins, Reginald "Ridge" McTaggart and his younger brother Marvin "Monkey-wrench" McTaggart.

"Be seated and hush up, now!" ordered Miss Tillman in her quiet but firm voice. "I don't want to have to growl at anyone."

The group calmed down remarkably at her tranquil display of authority, and she began delivering opening instructions. The McTaggart ʋoys squirmed in their front-row seats under her watchful scrutiny, and ɟid their best to look interested. Travis earnestly endeavored to take ɟetailed notes as the teacher turned her back on the class and strolled to ʰe expansive chalkboard. She had hardly reached her place and picked ɩp a piece of chalk when a mighty wad of wet, well-chewed paper ɩanded—plop!—smack in the middle of George Washington's forehead, ɩdhering to the glass like a giant bird dropping.

The teacher whirled like a fighting rooster, almost catching Monkey-wrench in the act as he settled innocently into his seat. Unfortunately for him, Miss Tillman was expert at observing the trajectory of such spit-laden projectiles, and she sensed the tell-tale rustle of clothes against the aggressor's seat. Though she hadn't seen the toss, she couldn't be easily fooled. She looked directly at Monkey-wrench, her terrible fiery eyes locked on him with a fierce but calm burn.

"Marvin, did you do that?"

"No, Ma'am," he replied solemnly, writhing ever so slightly under her intense scrutiny. After an uncomfortable pause, he finally added, "But I confess."

"You confess? You're saying you did it, then?"

"No, Ma'am. I confess Bean did it."

The whole class chuckled aloud, enough to completely convict Monkey-wrench. He was hustled away to the principal's office for administration of appropriate punishment. Eli Thompson never treated such incidents with anything less than capital seriousness, and his stern, inevitable wooden paddle stayed busy some days. This time poor Bubba missed taking the blame, but such scanty planning by his malicious cousins was far from the norm. Sometimes hapless Bean benefited from the fact that most teachers were wise to such nasty tactics by the McTaggart brothers. But more often he got undeserved punishment for those unmerciful McTaggart escapades.

The math lesson began in earnest, with Travis considerably ahead of the others because of his head start. Today's problems weren't that challenging, and seemed geared towards slower students, so he was soon finished. Monkey-wrench returned to his seat after a while, easing his tender backside into his desk gingerly. He was much more serious in demeanor than before, and began shuffling some papers as if working on his assignment. It wasn't long before Travis stared slightly upward, bored, and began counting innumerable whirls of asbestos fibers in one of the ceiling tiles. Shortly, Mr. Thompson appeared at the door and nodded acknowledgement to Miss Tillman. He then pointed at Travis and motioned him outside into the hallway.

"Got a special job for you. Come on down to the office," he whispered as Travis approached the open door.

"Yes, sir," replied the boy as he stepped into the hallway. He already knew what would be required. Mr. Thompson always sent him to the bank sometime during the week with a cigar box stuffed with cash. Indian Park School accumulated money from a variety of sources, such as lunch money, basketball gate receipts, and money collected by classes from fundraisers and the like. Since the bank was open only from 9:00 A.M. until noon, it was often difficult for the principal to get away to make a deposit. Mr. Thompson always told Travis exactly how much money was in the box so he could be sure the bank receipt was correct before returning to school. It was a tremendous honor to be entrusted with such a task, and it gave the boy a wonderful sense of pride.

"Today is an especially big amount, Travis, after last night's big ball game. There's $2,223.45 in the box. As always, straight to the bank and straight back."

"Yes, sir," said Travis solemnly, tucking the box under his arm as he turned to go. He headed out the front door and down the street, went left by the Methodist church, took a shortcut down a rough stretch of railroad tracks, and then made a left to the bank. It took only a few minutes, and it was nice to be outside, if only briefly. The sun was shining, it was a very warm day for early winter, and his feet fairly glided from cross tie to cross tie as he finished his shortcut.

In front of the institution, Banker Barksdale was talking to Gordy Chalmers, a somewhat retarded man whose entire family seemed to be similarly afflicted to some degree. Banker was his usual dapper self, white hair immaculately groomed, standing tall and stately in his expensive business suit. Gordy had on a worn, torn pair of overalls and a red plaid shirt, and his belly stuck out so far there was no way he could see his toes apart from some degree of contortion. He sported a minimum of three days' growth of beard, and a grease-stained John Deere cap sat sideways on his balding head. His ears were so big that they looked like the doors of a car left wide open, and prominent tufts of dark hair grew from each of his ear canals and from his nostrils.

The boy ascended weathered concrete steps into the building, but he could still hear Banker and Gordy talking outside as he waited for his turn with the teller. In front of him, to his surprise, were broad shoulders belonging to Dead Bird Wilson, the older of the two Wilson boys who lived next door to him. The youth stared straight ahead, and thus he had no idea that Travis was behind him. Dead Bird had quit school long ago, and as far as anyone knew he didn't hold a steady job or have any reason to do any banking. He and his brother Razz could have been identical twins, except that Dead Bird had darker hair. Both brothers kept their locks long and greasy, with luxurious sideburns lapping down well past the corner of the mouth. Dead Bird was dressed in ratty, ill-fitting pants and a hand-me-down shirt with a flower pattern, all of it dirty and smelling of smoke and tobacco and sweat and stale beer. Nobody seemed to know the exact origin of the boys' names, except that Razz's real name was widely reputed to be Dewberry, a word distantly related to raspberry, and thus "Razz." Why someone would be called "Dead Bird" was anybody's guess, and nobody seemed to know if this were a nickname or an actual name.

Razz had recently been released from prison, after serving a ridiculously short term for an armed robbery at this very bank. Banker Barksdale had recognized him in the course of that heist, and had admonished him sternly and fearlessly that he should put away the gun lest he hurt somebody. Instead, Razz had fled in a stolen car with a small amount of cash, chased by a determined Banker Barksdale in his fleet Cadillac. Not a shot had been fired, and the Georgia State Patrol had cut Razz off before he even reached Cherokee City. He was already out on parole, but today he was nowhere to be seen.

Dead Bird was making some kind of transaction, the nature of which remained obscure to Travis. He watched the teller comply with the youth's request while listening, unavoidably, to an unabashed conversation just outside the open door.

"Gordy, why'd you take that ten dollars out of your account?" asked Banker, shamelessly inquisitive about every transaction that drew money away from his institution.

"Aw, Banker, ye a-a-always a-a-axe me w-w-why when I git money. I'-i'-i's fo' m'-m'-m' brother."

"Which one, Gordy? The one in the chain gang or the one in the asylum?"

"Th-th-th' one in th' 'sylum, Banker. 'E-'e-'e needs some money fo' a t-t-taxi ride nex' week."

"Hmph. Waste of money. He must be doing well if they're letting him come home."

"'E-'e-'e ain't comin' home. 'E-'e-'e's goin' in th' a-a-army."

"Now that makes me feel good," said Banker, heavy irony in his voice completely lost on Gordy. "How can he be going in the army if he's in the insane asylum?"

30

"W-w-well, B-b-banker, sometime 'e's might nigh normal, t-t-talks real good sense; an' 'en 'gin 'e ain't got no-no-no sense a-tall," said Gordy with great effort. He added as an afterthought, "Sometimes 'e ain't got n-n-no more sense'n ye got."

"Hmph," said Banker, turning to re-enter the bank. Travis had heard the whole conversation, and somehow he managed to hide most of his mirth as he greeted Banker. On hearing Travis' voice, Dead Bird Wilson whirled to face him, startling the boy so badly that he almost dropped the school cigar box.

"Whatchew doin' 'ere, squirt?" Dead Bird asked gruffly. "Ain't ye s'posed to be in school?"

"Doing a job for Mr. Thompson," replied Travis, struggling to maintain his composure as he looked into Dead Bird's glowering eyes. "How about you?"

"Now 'at ain't none o' yo' business, smarty-pants," said Dead Bird with a smirk as he tucked a fat envelope into a pocket. As he strode from the bank and started up the sidewalk, he added as an afterthought, "Tell 'at good-lookin' mama o' yorn hi."

The money safely deposited and the school's receipt tucked into the cigar box, Travis headed back, reversing his steps exactly and turning up the railroad tracks. He met a backwoods family, the Bennys, walking the convenient tracks to town. Travis knew them well, because he and Hank sometimes visited their backwoods home for a warm-up on cold days while squirrel hunting. Sometimes when hunting was good and their bag was full, they would give them a squirrel or two from their take. Mrs. Benny always went to town once a week, wearing the same print dress, walking awkwardly in black highheeled shoes and full-length white socks. It was a marvel to see her negotiate the irregular cross ties in such unwieldy footwear, but she managed it handily after years of practice. They greeted Travis warmly before proceeding on into town.

Approaching the left turn where he would leave the railroad tracks near the Methodist church, he was about to step onto rough back street pavement when a firm hand grabbed his left arm and flung him around. The cigar box bounced down into a gravel-strewn ditch, and that precious receipt fluttered out and began rolling with the breeze toward a dense tangle of frost-killed kudzu.

"Gotcha, squirt!" said Dead Bird Wilson, who held him in a hammerlock grip with his hands on the back of his neck. As he lifted Travis off the ground slightly, the smell of his body and clothes was overpowering. Razz Wilson now appeared as well, and he retrieved the cigar box and receipt. He scrutinized the piece of paper seriously as his brother controlled a terrified Travis in his vain struggle.

"Lot o' money ye wuz totin', kid. Too bad we wuzn't 'ere when ye wuz on yo' way t' th' bank."

"Turn me loose. I'll tell Mr. Thompson on you guys," said Travis, his voice quivering noticeably.

"'E can't do nothin' t' us. We don't go t' 'at school no mo'. Fack is, nobody kin tell us whut t' do. 'Ey kin brang on th' supertenner o' schools an' 'e can't say nothin' a-tall t' me. An' ye jes' better be keerful who ye tell anythin' 'bout 'is," said Dead Bird. His captive had finally ceased to struggle, the effort seeming hardly worth it in view of the vise-like hold of his adversary. Thoughts of mentioning Sheriff Hoke faded from Travis's mind as he realized that it would probably only incite these two.

"I seed ye watchin' Dead Bird in th' bank," said Razz. "Ye wuz mighty inner-ested, 'peer'd t' me. Ye didn' see nothin', did ye?"

"I saw Dead Bird get an envelope from the teller. That's all I saw. I swear it."

"Ye didn' see 'at, neither. Ye heah me? We wuzn' e'en at th' bank."

"You weren't at the bank?"

"We wuzn' at th' bank. An' don't ye fergit it," said Dead Bird, tightening his grip and lifting the boy higher as he emphasized his point.

"Okay, okay! Ye wuzn't at th' bank! An' I won't fergit it," he capitulated.

"An' ye better not crawfish on us, boy," said Dead Bird through clenched teeth.

The older Wilson boy released him and shoved him down onto hard, unyielding gravel between the iron tracks. Razz tossed the receipt at him, and once more it began rolling briskly toward the thick kudzu, while Travis scrambled to retrieve it. He recovered his cigar box as the malevolent pair climbed a steep red bank beside the railroad and disappeared.

CHAPTER 3

School days came and went with regularity, and winter dreariness gave way to glorious spring, then spring slowly turned to hot, hazy summer. was a lazy time of year for Travis, with school out of session and no much regular on his agenda. He kept busy mowing grass and making money doing odd jobs for the many elderly people in Indian Park. It was a pleasant time when he was able to set his own schedule and pass the summer doing pretty much as he pleased. He belonged to the Boy Scouts, and that weekly meeting was his only fixed event. He regularly met the bookmobile in the hamlet, and set a goal of reading two books week all summer.

The preacher was one person who never hired the boy for an paying job. The old man was an oddball of a person, though this was not an uncommon anomaly in the area. He lived just across the dusty road from the Jackson family, but slightly higher on the mountain. His name was Homer Holiday, and his wife was named "her," as far as anyone knew, since that term was the only one Homer ever used when referring to her. Homer was a true believer, and he wouldn't hesitate to tell you so. He was what was known as a "holy roller," and he subscribed to a more odd philosophy, claiming to believe every word of the Bible, and then some. Whether he was actually a preacher or not Travis Jackson couldn't tell. Nobody the boy knew had ever heard him preach a sermon, and he had heard that several local churches had expelled Mr. Holiday for saying "amen" too loudly and too often. But since Homer himself insisted that he had been "called to preach," it was impossible to dismiss such a possibility altogether.

Travis liked to banter with local old folks, and it was time for his almost-nightly walk. He told his mother goodbye and strolled across the dirt lane to Homer's house.

Homer stood as straight as a flagpole, and he had broad shoulders and a muscular build. In his younger days he doubtless had been quite

34

physical specimen. Even in his seventies he showed every indication of strength and durability. He was always clean-shaven, and took considerable pride in keeping his straight razor honed to a fine edge. His face was round and he had thin, fragile lips, as well as a petite nose for a man his size. His hair was still only slightly thin but was heavily streaked with gray. Homer's eyebrows curled upward and outward in most curious fashion, and looked almost as if he had used some kind of treatment to mold them, though such would have been entirely out of character for him. He walked with an arm-waving hop, apparently more from habit than from any lameness. He was thrifty and resourceful, despite his peculiarities, and he was always ready to share. If one needed anything at all, Homer Holiday probably had it, and would let you take it freely. If he didn't have a particular item on hand, he knew exactly what was the best possible substitute, and he gladly gave advice on how to use it.

Today Homer was dressed, as usual, in his worn overalls and high-top shoes, and he wore a threadbare plaid shirt. A patch from a chicken feed sack was meticulously stitched onto one knee of his trousers, and the other knee was close to needing the same treatment. He was busily digging in his expansive garden when Travis arrived. The preacher was stooped in the midst of luxurious potato plants, and he had a generous bucket filled to the brim with fat, brown spuds, and fresh earth clung to each one. He stood up briskly to face his neighbor boy, looking as fit as kudzu on a power pole, with tall, ripe corn towering behind him as a backdrop.

"Evenin', Mr. Holiday," the boy greeted the preacher warmly. "How are you today?"

"Hurtin', son. Don't ax me how I feel, jes' ax me whur I'm hurtin'," came the familiar reply.

"I'm sorry," said Travis, trying to exude genuine concern. "At least your garden looks great."

"Fair t' middlin', son, fair t' middlin'. 'Twon't matter much if'n i grows fum 'ere t' Cherokee City if'n 'is cancer on m' lip keeps a-eatin on me. An' th' doctor bills jes' keep a-pilin'. Got t' go t'morry, fack is An' take 'er, too. She's a-hurtin' might nigh bad as me. Oh, I'm hurtin'!"

He said this last phrase so loudly and with so much feeling that the boy jumped involuntarily, startled. He quickly recovered his composure and he hoped the preacher hadn't noticed.

"You said you got some new medicine," observed the boy, recalling what Homer had told him a few days before. "Didn't it help?"

"Nary a bit, son. Ner 'ers neither. Like spittin' on a fores' fire. An 'em pills cost more'n ol' Solomon kin pay. I guess we'll jes' hafta hurt th' way 'ey cost. I'm a-headin' in now, son. Come on in an' say hello t' 'er befo' it's too late."

Travis Jackson loved to be invited in, since the whole layout was fascinating to him. They walked together to Homer's wooden frame house, which in summer was surrounded by growing plants, particularly a vast array of colorful flowers. The bountiful garden almost surrounded the dwelling, and featured more than a dozen varieties of vegetables growing, with sweet potatoes and corn comprising the largest quantity An ancient Chevrolet truck was parked between the house and garden, and was the machine that provided horsepower for cultivation. By way of Homer's unconventional genius, this old vehicle had been stripped down to its frame and modified so that the two rear tires were oversized for more efficient plowing and pulling. It had become a makeshift tractor, Homer's unique creation, and hardly anyone could so much as figure out how to crank its engine except him.

In the back yard were two major structures of significance. There was a garage, which was stuffed with a lifetime's accumulation of rusty tools, hardware, wire, cans of all descriptions, boxes of unknown content, as well as hundreds of fruit jars and other nondescript glass containers, many of them containing screws, nails, nuts, and bolts of all sizes. Rolled into one corner was a giant ball of string to which Homer added at every opportunity. This collection of twine was so heavy that one could scarcely budge it without assistance. There were also several piles of scrap metal, consisting of material scavenged from all around the area and separated according to its type. Each kind commanded a specific price from the scrap dealer in Cherokee City, some being more valuable and other varieties less so.

The second building was a long, low wood shed, which overflowed with enough cured, split firewood to last an overly optimistic person several lifetimes. To this immense supply of fuel Homer added constantly, almost with pathological fervor.

Indoors was "her" domain, but it was much the same, with stores of various wares in every nook. Her collections consisted of different categories of items, such as jars of preserves and canned vegetables of varying ages, glasses filled with buttons or pins, and enough surplus army blankets to outfit a batallion. A woodburning stove in the living area stayed merry and hot during winter, and in fact it was so warm in the room that it was impossible for an average person to remain there for very long. Dusty pictures hung on every wall, presumably faces of family and friends, though none of them were familiar to Travis, because hardly anyone except him ever visited the Holiday home these days. The main hallway had a big closet full of shelves, containing a vast collection of prescription medications stacked to the ceiling. Some of it was prescribed for Homer, and some for her, and they actually took some of it.

On entering they encountered a familiar musty smell, and found Mrs. Holiday rocking in the living room, holding a pan on her lap. The container was full of green beans that she was breaking and "stringing." She first snapped off one end of each bean, stripped a long, tough fiber from one side, then left it attached while she broke off the remaining end and stripped the string off in the other direction. She then snapped each de-stringed morsel into three or four pieces and dropped them in to her pan. She then picked up another bean and repeated the process. Her fingers flew so fast they were like a machine, and prepared beans were piling up quickly. Doubtless they would end up in fruit jars in the back storage room or garage, where there were already at least a thousand quarts of beans and other vegetables left over from years past. Alternatively, the beans might be threaded onto strings and sun-dried to make "leather britches," a durable mountain staple that was slowly being lost in a dawning era of canneries and home freezers.

"How are you, Mrs. Holiday?" asked Travis, suppressing an impulse to mischievously chuckle.

"Hurtin', honey, hurtin'. Goin' t' th' doctor 'gin t'morry wi' him. Don't really 'speck no improvin', though."

She seemed to redouble her attention to the pile of beans, while Homer opened the closet door and once more revealed their vast treasure trove of prescription bottles. He opened one bottle and popped a pill into his mouth, then carried another to his wife. Using a dipper, he filled a glass from the well bucket on the table, swallowed one long gulp, and then passed the glass to her. She likewise downed her medicine, and then wiped her mouth with one corner of her colorful apron.

Travis was most careful not to offend the old couple over their plethora of physical complaints, though he sometimes couldn't help but be amused. Despite their hypochondriac ways, both were deeply sincere and were excellent neighbors. They also seemed to possess strength of character and a fondness for one another that transcended mere physical things, and somehow the boy sensed a need to respect them.

Travis's younger brother Bobby was much less diplomatic, and often imitated the anguished cries of the elderly couple in their distress. He did so in such loud fashion that sometimes his mocking sounds clearly carried across the dirt road, so that the Holidays couldn't miss hearing him. For some days after any such incident, Homer would cease to speak or acknowledge his neighbors as he passed by on the road, or even look toward the Jackson house. Ruth Jackson always roundly colded Bobby for his indiscretion every time she heard him, but his delight in mimicking the preacher was such that no punishment was sufficient to indefinitely deter him. Invariably, though, Homer seemed to eventually either forgive or forget, and subsequently he would resume his normal pattern of behavior, including an occasional sharp "Oh" or "I'm hurtin'" ringing out from his direction.

Farther up the dirt road was Hank McCard's home. Hank was a retired chicken farmer, a vocation that he had pursued for much of his life. There were still a half dozen chicken houses on his small parcel of land, but these days a son-in-law, his daughter Gracie's husband Teddy, tended them. Hank had raised millions of broiler chickens in his time, and in the process he had developed an extreme level of disdain for chickens in general, but particularly for chickens as food. His main interest in life was squirrel hunting and squirrel dogs, and it was this passion that drew him and Travis Jackson together more than anything else. Almost every evening in summertime, Travis ambled a short quarter mile down the dusty road to sit on Hank's front porch and just talk.

Tonight was such a summer evening, and when the boy left the Holiday house he headed straight for the McCard's. As always Hank sat in a rocking chair with his legs crossed, rhythmically raising and lowering a crossed leg as he rocked. His joints were stiffened such that his swaying foot was pointed acutely upward, fairly locked in that position. Hank was in his mid-to-late seventies, tall but somewhat stooped by age and hard work, yet he still had a full head of hair. This latter fact was hard to confirm, though, because he seldom removed his broad-brimmed felt hat until it was time for bed. Travis had seen him lift it to shield his eyes from the sun while seeking a treed squirrel, so he knew the whole story. The old man's nose was as hooked as a beak on a red-tailed hawk, and his eyes were sky blue, deep-set, and penetrating. He was naturally leaner and lankier than his son, H.K., in part a matter of metabolism but also likely because he had quit drinking whiskey years ago. He always wore faded overalls and a long-sleeved shirt, no matter the weather or time of year. His left cheek was perpetually distended by a wad of chewing tobacco, a feature as invariable as any other part of his anatomy.

The house was neatly painted, and the yard was freshly mowed. Heat from the summer sun was fading, and there was a pleasant breeze blowing from the direction of an old burned forest across the road. A bobwhite quail called from deep broomsedge near the edge of the burn, obviously seeking a mate. Hank threw up his hand in acknowledgement as the boy crossed the yard.

"Evening, Mr. McCard," said Travis respectfully as he approached the porch.

"Evenin', son," Hank replied, spitting tobacco juice into a can and reaching for a kerchief in his pocket as he spoke. He motioned the boy to a wooden swing suspended from rafters next to him as he wiped his mouth and kept on rocking.

"How's H.K.? Getting back any use of that arm yet?"

"Some. Ne'er be good as new, I reckin. Yo' mama an' 'em all okay?"

"Fine. I saw Mr. Holiday on my way over. He's still hurtin'."

"Yep. An' don't hesitate t' tell ye 'bout it, neither. Some preacher 'e is. Used t' spend th' night down in 'em woods o'er 'ere, befo' th' big fire, prayin' loud as a dog treein' a 'coon. Sounded jes' like one, fack is. Onliest good thang 'bout 'at fire, 'e don't do 'at no mo'. 'At, an' all th' blackberries 'at grows 'ere now."

"Ever hear him preach, Mr. McCard?"

"'Im? Naw. Don't care much fer preachin' m'se'f, nohow. An' if'n 'e's a preacher, th' woods is full o' 'em."

"Do you think he's really sick, Mr. McCard? He said he saw their doctor again this week."

"'Im? Naw. I reckin 'ey'll have t' knock 'at ol' coot in th' head Jedgment Day. Looks sounder'n ary dollar t' me," said Hank as he once more spit into his can. "Works all day in 'at garden o' 'is when it's a hunnert degrees an' 'e's wetter'n a possum crossin' th' creek. An' moanin' an' groanin' all th' while. Prob'ly smells like a mule 'at's been rode hard an' put away wet. 'Is wife's th' one 'at's sick, in my 'pinion, puttin' up wi' th' likes o' 'im fer forty-odd years."

"Yeah, I guess you're right," said the boy, resignation in his voice. He knew better than to try and change Hank's mind on anything. It was better to change the subject.

"How are Bruno and Spot?"

"Fine as frog's hair. Best pair o' squirrel dogs I've had in a 'coon's age. But I'll ne'er fergit 'at cur dog way back yonder—ol' Rowdy wuz 'is name. Man, whut a dog 'at wuz. I wuz workin' at th' sawmill at th' time. Did I e'er tell ye 'bout 'at? I worked fer fifty cents a day, and I had nine miles t' go t' work. An' I had two ways t' git 'ere—I could wawk, OR," he always paused and emphasized the first OR, and sometimes he took time to spit again, "Or I could run. An' if'n I wuz a minute late, it'd show up on m' paycheck. Mighty tough on me an' Maggie in 'em days."

The boy nodded in agreement and manufactured an extreme degree of wonder at this oft-repeated revelation. He didn't know how much of it to believe, but surely there had to be a grain of truth, at least, in the tale. There had indeed been some hard economic times back then. He'd heard his own grandfather talk about it. And old Hank could still walk mighty well for his age, perhaps a positive residual of his long-ago treks to the job.

"Ye young-uns got no idee how bad it wuz back in 'em days. Ridin' everwhur ye go nowadays in fancy cars, school buses pickin' ye up at th' door, an' th' like. Why, me 'n' Maggie wawked everwhur we went th' fust ten years we wuz married. Draggin' Elmer and H.K. and th' gals along, too, adder 'ey got born'd. Mighty good thang I had a .22 pump rifle and a li'l' change t' buy bullets, or we'd 'ave sho' starved plum t' death."

"You ate a lot of squirrel back then, huh?"

"Yep. Had t'," said Hank as he spit again. "Still do. Ye let 'em city slickers eat all 'em chickens we raise 'roun' heah, and I'll stick t' th' good meat. A squirrel is a clean critter, partic'lar 'bout whut 'e picks up an' eats. But a chicken's wusser'n a catfish 'bout scavengin'. Soon as eat worms, maggots, whutever, e'en each other, as not."

"My mama's fried chicken tastes pretty good, Mr. McCard."

"Don't matter none 'bout taste. It's whut ye puttin' inside yo' innards 'at matters. I'd sooner eat a piece o' mad dog 'an eat a piece o' chicken. I've seed 'em gather 'em up half sick an' load 'em fer th' plant, an' e'en toss in one er two might nigh dead. Foreman'd say 'ey'll make soup, toss 'em on in. If'n one o' 'em birds is s' twisted 'is bill's pointin' t'wards 'is tail, 'ey'll still crate 'im up an' ship 'im out. An' folks whut eats 'im ne'er knows th' dif'rence. Nope, sooner eat a piece o' mad dog 'an a piece o' chicken, m'se'f."

"It's a good thing you had such a good dog back then, so you didn't have to depend on chickens to feed everybody. Tell me about that cur dog, Mr. McCard. Was he as good as Bruno? I can't even imagine a dog as good as Bruno, or even one as good as Spot, for that matter."

"'Im? Naw, Bruno ain't nothin' compared t' ol' Rowdy. Ol' Rowdy used t' stay under th' porch, an' nothin' ner nobody wuz comin' in 'is yard lessen 'e 'lowed it. An' 'e'd tree anythin' wi' hair, be it squirrel, 'possum, 'coon, or man. Didn' make no matter t' 'im. An' woe be t' th' varmi't whut can't clim' quick an' well, 'e's a goner fer sho'. Yep, sho' do miss ol' Rowdy."

"What happened to him?"

"Got old, like me an' Maggie. An' slow. Mailman runned over 'im, by accident, 'e claimed. 'Ey ne'er did like one 'nother, 'im an' 'at mailman, s' I ne'er wuz sho'. Mighty fine dog, though, ne'er be 'nother 'un like 'im."

"I'd like to have a dog like that. Then I could walk right past the Wilson place and they'd be afraid to say anything, with a real cur dog walking beside me. Right, Mr. McCard?"

"'Em? Naw, 'ey'd be skeered o' a dog like 'at, fer sho'. I think 'ey's purty skeered o' lots o' thangs, anyhow. 'Ey's jes' all show. Don't be 'fraid o' 'em, boy."

"Well, they're scary sometimes. And strange," he added. He thought about telling the old man about his encounter with the two Wilson boys the past winter, but he'd promised he wouldn't tell anyone, and he hadn't. But it was tempting to break his vow. "And when my Mama goes by there, they sing 'Hey Good-Lookin' real loud and scary. They can't carry a tune in a bucket, but you can tell what they're trying to sing. They hoot and holler at Mama like that every time we drive by. Old Poss and his boys, too. And they're always drinking and spitting..."

The old man reached for his tin can and spit into it again, then wiped his chin with his handkerchief.

"'At beer 'ey kin have, an' 'at so-called singin', too, fer 'at matter. But don't go throwin' off none on spittin', son. Nary a thang wrong with a little chaw now an' 'en."

"I guess it's all right if you use a can like you do. The Wilsons just spit all over the porch and their front yard. I've heard they even spit on the walls inside their house, too."

"'Ey do. Been in it one time, when ol' Tot had a brand new young-un way back. Took 'at young-un some apples, I did, an' some peppermint candy. An' some squirrel dumplins Maggie made. 'Em dumplins smelt mighty good, but in 'at place 'ey wuz at odds wi' a passel o' stronger stuff. Smelt like a outhouse in 'ere, an' d'reckly 'em dumplins smelt th' same way. 'Ey et 'em anyhow, jes' wolfed 'em down like a dog eatin' biscuits. An' sho' 'nuff, 'ey wuz chawin' juice all o'er th' walls, runnin' down t' th' floor. 'Ey don't need no spittin' cans, don't reckin."

"That's awful. I went in their yard once, taking a shortcut to my grandpa's house. But usually I go way around through the woods. I can't help but be mighty leery of them. You don't think they'd hurt anybody?"

"'Em? Naw, nary a hurtful bone in 'em, 'ceptin' maybe in ol' Razz. He's got a mite o' mean streak. 'Ey's a quare bunch, but 'ey's mos'ly all tawk. Now ol' Runt Mayberry, he'd cut out yo' liver 'n' ne'er thank twict 'bout it. Don't mess wi' 'im, son. E'en ol' Hoke Hatfield won't go t' 'is place by 'isse'f."

The boy shuddered a little on thinking of Mayberry. Tot Wilson's brother lived down by the railroad tracks in a ramshackle, unpainted wooden house. He had a common-law wife and maybe a dozen kids crammed tightly into a three-room dwelling. The boy and Hank had run into the disagreeable character on one of their squirrel hunts, far back in remote lumber company woods, early in last year's squirrel season. Mayberry's dogs had treed the same squirrel as Bruno and Spot, and the whole pack had been feuding and growling like lions arguing over a kill. Mayberry had already reached the tree before Travis and Hank arrived, and he might have shot Bruno and Spot had they not showed up when they did. He made it clear to them that this was his squirrel, and they should call off their dogs. He'd said he had a passel of young-uns to feed, and he needed that squirrel more than any old man and boy. It hadn't been so much what he said as the way he said it, with a chilling tone in his voice that left no doubt he was grim determined. Travis remembered clearly how seriously old Hank had taken his words. They had pulled the McCard dogs back while Mayberry shot the squirrel, which had turned out to be infested with "wolves," or botfly larvae, and was thus by most accounts inedible. Mayberry had kept it, anyway, scowling that the detestable larvae under the skin "jes' makes more dumplins."

"Say, boy, 'ey tells me ye gonna go t' a dif'rent school now."

Travis snapped his thoughts back to the present conversation.

"Yes, sir, when school starts I'll be in ninth grade in Cherokee City. Long bus ride every day."

"Tarnation, 'at's a shame. I be dog. Hard t' git home in time fer any huntin', wi' s' fur t' go."

"We've got Saturdays. And sometimes maybe I'll be home early enough."

"Well, we got time t' study it some, anyhow. An' it's time t' pick blackberries an' leave th' squirrels alone fer th' summer, too. 'Ey needs a break, same's us."

The door creaked open, and Maggie McCard's bright, weathered face appeared. She had a head of white hair and an ever-present smile, and she looked unusually tired. Travis rose to his feet and greeted her, and she returned his friendly salutation.

"Time for supper, Hank."

"Yes, ma'am," said Hank respectfully. "Care t' eat, son? Maggie's th' bes' cook in Cherokee County—er might nigh any county, fer 'at matter."

"I know that's right, Mr. McCard. But no, sir, thanks anyway. Got to be home in a minute. Want to go fill a bucket with blackberries tomorrow?"

"Sho' 'nuff. Early, befo' it gits too hot. Maggie makes mighty fine blackberry jam, an' th' finest pies 'at'll make yo' mouf water a gallon. Brang a big bucket, 'at burn over 'ere is jes' packed wi' big, ripe 'uns. An' it's crawlin' wi' ticks an' chiggers, too, but I got plenty o' kerosene t' keep 'em off'n us. "

"I'll be here. See you then."

As he walked home, the boy contemplated the conversation. Most of the talk had been conventional, normal, even repetitive. But the Runt Mayberry information had been a new twist, and he found it a little unsettling. Runt had a reputation as a squirrel hunter of highest order, but he was doubtless a mean and difficult man, too. But Travis had never thought of him as being actually dangerous, the way Hank did. He recalled numerous verbal altercations with Mayberry's eldest son, Mutt, who was as unfriendly as people came. But he had always thought the Wilsons to be a much bigger threat.

Things aren't always as they seem, he noted. He was still plenty uncomfortable with his next-door neighbors, but he'd be powerful careful when it came to dealing with any of Runt Mayberry's clan.

CHAPTER 4

A heavy dew greeted Travis as he crossed his yard the next morning, heading for the McCard place. By the time he stepped from the grassy yard into the road, his clod-busters were already soaked, and he began picking up dirt from the dry ground that quickly accumulated into a sticky heaviness underfoot. He stamped his feet to dislodge some of it. Soon he was at the McCard house, where Hank was already on the back porch, readying his bucket. He greeted the boy warmly.

"Mornin', son. Git on up 'ere an' rub some o' 'is kerosene on yo' shoes an' britches legs. An' put some on yo' shirtsleeves, too, an' 'round yo' neck, er else 'ey'll be ticks in yo' armpits. An' chiggers, too, th' li'l' devils. An' dab a li'l' roun' yo' waist, too, jes' in case. It won't hurt nothin', jes' stinks a mite."

"Okay," said Travis, complying with all instructions. In a few minutes both of them smelled like a couple of lifelong diesel mechanics after a hard day's work. Shortly they sauntered across the road and began crossing the jungle-like burn, a hundred acres of scorched land that was cut with numerous wide erosion ditches, punctuated irregularly by blackened dead snags, and covered with chest-deep secondary growth of all kinds. Near a small branch stream there were tangles of blackberry vines, so thick one could only with difficulty reach the most luxurious berries. The fruit was hanging thick, some of it more than an inch long, deep black in color, and so sweet to the taste that Travis had a hard time dropping his pickings into the bucket instead of eating them. He more or less alternated eating and gathering until his stomach was satisfied.

Hank and the boy worked the easiest places first, those along the narrow trail, but when these were combed it became necessary to push deeper. A foot raised into the tangle of briars could push them aside, one cane at a time, but great care had to be exercised in order to avoid the numerous viscious thorns. When a new opening was created, the picker could step forward and once more begin reaping the bounty of ripe blackberries. This scenario would be repeated until both of them had full buckets. An ever-present danger was wasps and hornets, which loved to build their round paper nests under the impervious shelter of thick bushes. By this time of year, a wasp nest was more than four inches in diameter and held over a hundred wasps, all of them armed missiles ready to explode into action against any unlucky intruder. Travis had been stung badly the year before, so he was acutely aware of the malicious insects. He checked carefully before collapsing each successive promising location, and avoided one large nest by spotting it early and moving in another direction.

"Mr. McCard, watch out right here," he called to his friend. "Wasps! And a whole wad of them, at that!"

"Good eye, boy. I seed one o'er 'ere, too. 'Ey's always right in th' bes' berries. Shoulda brung a mite o' gas t' pitch on 'em."

"Maybe. Next best thing is to just avoid them," replied Travis as he continued picking in his new location.

His hands flew and his bucket was rapidly getting heavy with ripe, juicy fruit. He was so intent on pulling choice berries and keeping one eye out for wasps that he almost forgot that there were other dangers as well. He stepped forward slightly, and something thick, firm, and agile moved underneath his foot, startling him so badly he dropped his bucket, sending berries flying. He knew immediately that it was a snake, and that he could be in grave danger. Almost simultaneously with the tactile sensation, the frightening whir of an agitated rattlesnake added to his sense of terror. He was afraid to move and even fearful that speaking might worsen the situation. He looked down slowly, and he could see the coiled menace, its head and tail held aloft, and his foot just abutting the creature's thick midsection. The slightest additional annoyance and Travis would not be able to avoid its lightening-fast, deadly bite.

"Son, 'at's a ol' rattler I heah a-singin'," said Hank in matter-of-fact fashion. He glanced at the boy, who was standing, perfectly motionless, staring at the ground, his complexion drained of all color, and the old man knew instantly the boy was in mortal danger.

"I'm on him, Mr. McCard!" said Travis in a terrified whisper. "If I move my foot at all he'll strike! I can see his big old head and his rattles, too!"

"Now don't ye dare move nothin', son. Let 'at ol' boy go on a-singing fer now. I'll git a stick an' distrack th' varmi't. 'E won't hurt ye less'n ye move, s' make like ye wuz a squirrel an' 'at snake's got ye treed."

"What choice do I have?" came the boy's terse, muffled whisper.

"A mighty sore leg, fer one thang. But it ain't gon' happen."

"I hope you're right," said Travis, still fixing his gaze on his adversary. The snake's wicked diamondback pattern glistened with dew, and the head swayed back and forth slightly as the rattles continued to buzz. The boy prayed out loud for God to help him while Hank looked for exactly the right tool to use. He felt himself calm perceptibly as he prayed ever so briefly, though it seemed like the moment would never end. Finally, the old man returned and eased up slowly behind Travis like a cat stalking a bird. He had a stout stick in hand, and he had wrapped his handerchief tightly around one end. He took the makeshift device and stuck it near the snake's head, moving it in tantalizing fashion, probing and jabbing the creature's body ever so slightly.

"Now when 'at varmi't strikes, ye put ye'se'f in full reverse, boy," counseled Hank quietly. "Watch an' be ready. 'Is ol' rattler ain't done us no harm, an' 'e sho' 'nuff could o' bit a chunk out'n ye. Fer bein' a good snake, 'e gits t' live. Now watch close an' be ready."

Hank teased the snake more aggressively now, waving his decoy nearer and nearer the undulating head, interposing his tool between the business end of the snake and the Travis' leg. With amazing swiftness the triangular head flashed forward, and long, curved fangs buried deep into Hank's cloth. Travis backpedaled as fast as his legs would move, stumbling and falling into the briars in the process. Hank lifted the snake, still impinged on the cloth-wound stick, and flung it a dozen feet deeper into the blackberry thicket. Its singing rattles ceased, and the animal beat a quick retreat for safer territory.

"Wow, that was close!" said Travis jubilantly as he picked himself up from his sticky repose. Hank extended a hand to help him up, and they had to adjust the position of some thorn-laden canes so he could safely stand. He had some pretty nasty scratches, but no major injuries otherwise. As his breathing normalized and he shook himself off while taking stock of his condition, he added, "Thanks, Mr. McCard! Whew!"

"Any time, son. Bes' t' jes avoid 'em, er else ye could end up one-legged er worse. Knowed a feller one time whut lost 'is leg t' a rattler like 'at un. An' 'nothern at th' sawmill jes plain died fum a bite, way back 'ere. Keep one eye out fer wasps, 'nothern on th' ground, and pick 'em berries wi' whut e'er ye got lef' o'er. 'Ere, le's gather 'ese spilled berries back into yo' bucket."

Both of them stooped to the task, but Travis stared off in the direction the snake had retreated, hoping it would not return. Everything was now clear.

"I can't believe I actually stepped on a rattler. I usually see them and avoid them, but that one was hidden under the bushes. It doesn't pay to put your feet where you can't see," observed Travis as they worked.

"Son, ye done right good not t' lose yo' senses fum bein' skeered. If'n ye had, ye'd be bit t' th' quick right now. Keep 'at in yo' noggin when thangs git tight, an more'n likely ye'll come out on th' long end o' th' stick. Ye heah?"

"I will, Mr. McCard," said Travis, still staring into the impenetrable thicket. "Man, I've never been that close to a live rattler."

"'Ey's a higher power watchin' o'er ye, boy. A higher power. Fack is I ne'er seed a man step on one o' 'em critters an' git away scot clean, neither. Yep, had t' be a higher power watchin' o'er ye, son. 'At ol' boy wuz under 'ere catchin' rats an' sich vermin whut wuz eatin' dropped berries. 'Ey's one er two 'roun' ev'ry blackberry patch. Ye jes' stack 'at in yo' head an' learn y'se'f a mighty big lesson. An' ye'll git lots more'n jes' berries out'n 'is pickin' trip."

The two of them cleaned up most of Travis' spilled fruit, then finished filling both their buckets. Travis checked himself over as he worked, and discovered that most of the scratches from the wicked briars were on his arms, although there was also a long red line on one cheek. None of the marks were particularly deep. The boy pondered the big rattlesnake endlessly, along with his friend's sage advice, as he kept one eye warily on the ground. He was naturally relieved, even elated, that he had avoided a devastating injury, so his abrasions seemed insignificant. Somehow, too, his gladness of heart went far deeper than his avoidance of lasting physical damage.

Irreverant Hank McCard had expressed belief in a "higher power" three times. It was the closest to a religious comment Travis had ever heard from the old man.

As they walked home swinging pails filled to the brim with luscious blackberries, Travis kept a watchful vigil for any more snakes that might be stretched across the narrow trail. And he pondered everything Hank had said in the aftermath of that close call.

CHAPTER 5

It was a hot morning in late June, the kind of day when the air is sticky and tombstone still, and a relentless climbing sun threatened to make it increasingly uncomfortable. Travis glanced across the dirt road, which was still billowing a cloud of dust from a passing automobile, and noticed the preacher readying his ancient tractor. He had attached jumper cables between his old car and the tractor, a necessity in preparing to start it, and shortly the clatter of an antiquated engine could be heard as it roared to life. The garden was already plowed and planted, cultivated and done, except for minor weeding and final harvesting, so Homer Holiday obviously had something else in mind.

Travis called to his mother that he was going to see Mr. Holiday, and she gave permission by her silence. He encountered the old man working in his garage, wearing a sweat-stained felt hat that was his constant headcover. He was always putting the ragged headpiece on and taking it off in somewhat nervous fashion. His limp was a minor hindrance, and he seemed to be tireless despite this annoying ailment. Working all day beneath a hot sun never seemed to bother him in the least, and he was amazingly energetic when it came to duties involving home and garden. He had never worked at "public work," as he called it, but somehow he had enough income from somewhere to get by. He spoke first when he saw the boy approaching.

"Mornin', boy. How's it wi' ye?" asked the preacher, speaking loudly over the din of the engine.

"Fine, Mr. Holiday. How are you?" Travis shouted back.

"Hurtin', son, hurtin'. Don't ax me how I feel, jes' ax me whur I'm hurtin'."

"Where you hurtin', Mr. Holiday?"

"Everwhur. M' back, m' hip, m' legs. Las' night m' arm started actin' up again. And 'is cancer on m' lip is eatin' me alive, 'cordin' t' th' doctor. Oh, I'm hurtin'," he said, putting a little extra emphasis on the "Oh."

"I'm sorry, Mr. Holiday," said Travis, trying to appear genuinely concerned. "How's Mrs. Holiday?"

"Hurtin' too. Doctor says in 'er state she ain't got long. Got 'er some mo' o' 'at awful 'spensive medicine yestiddy, but so fur it ain't he'pin' 'er none a-tall. Doctors is takin' all we got 'n' 'en some. 'Em an' th' drug store."

"Sorry, Mr. Holiday," Travis repeated. He turned toward the rumbling machine and pointed at it, asking over its noise, "Why did you start up your tractor?"

"Got t' go t' th' dump. Th' city dumped three-four times 'is pas' week, and I got t' check it out befo' some scoundrel rifles through it fust. Wan' t' come along wi' me, boy?"

"Oh, wow. I'd like to. But I'll have to ask Mama. Be right back."

"No hurry, son. Got t' load m' tools."

The proposition sounded enticing to Travis. He had never spent any time rummaging at the town dump, but he had passed by it many times, and delving into it was something he had always wanted to do. His mother was less than enthusiastic, but she gave reluctant permission. Homer Holiday was a careful man, his idiosyncrasies notwithstanding, and her son needed masculine company. She would be glad when Christmas rolled around, when her husband would be home for a time, but for now even Homer Holiday was an improvement over some of her son's frequent companions. Very shortly the preacher had his gear aboard, whereupon man and boy climbed into the contraption.

Down the dirt road they traveled, Travis riding out repeated bumps while seated on the hard wooden bed of the modified truck. There were no shock absorbers or springs, so he could feel an electric-like jolt each time they bounced. Dust boiled up through cracks between the planks, but thankfully their speed was slow enough to hold it to a minimum. They scooted past Indian Park Boy Scout hut, crossed the only stretch of pavement between them and their destination, and then continued another mile and a half down a shady, tree-lined road. You could smell the site long before they reached it, a powerful stench of decay becoming stronger as they neared. Soon they were surrounded by mounds of nondescript trash of all kinds, some of it recently bulldozed under, but much of it still undisturbed and easily accessible. Homer parked his vehicle near the largest, freshest mound, and shut down its growling motor. The pair then dismounted and began to survey for available goodies.

There were myriad paper bags filled with reeking household garbage, everything from fish bones and chicken scraps to rotting potato peelings. Most of the fragile containers had burst and spilled already, victims of junkyard dogs, raccoons, and other scavengers. A couple of beat-up, defunct appliances could be seen amid waist-deep rubble, and several discarded automobile tires lay in various states of disarray. Broken furniture abounded and protruded at odd angles from the refuse. There were discarded magazines and newspapers lying all about, most of them well scrambled and distastefully scattered. At one end of the dump a fire burned, adding pungent smoke to the assault on one's senses. An idle yellow bulldozer was parked well away from the smouldering blaze, but nobody had apparently been there that day to repile or bury anything. Part of the trash mound already had a thick top covering of dirt, but the freshest and best had been left mostly unmolested, just as it had come from the trash truck.

"'Ere's a fine piece o' lunyum, boy. 'Ey pay four, maybe five times as much a pound fer 'is as fer arn. An' 'ese 'ere ignition blinds'll be good as new when I put 'nother pull cord on 'em. Don't need none in m' winders at home, but I know somebody'll give a purty penny fer 'ese."

They worked every pile, pulling out anything that might have value and loading it into the truck bed. It was a fascinating adventure in discovery for the boy, and he marveled at the quantity and quality of discarded merchandise. A big brass bedstead was partially covered with dirt and debris, and the preacher used his vehicle to pull it free from its imprisonment, only slightly abraded and bent.

"Jes' a little damaged, 'n' if'n I can't sell it as a bedstead it'll go on th' brass pile. Sometimes a li'l' damage don't hurt somethin's price all 'at much. After all, we's all damaged goods anyhow, right, son?"

"What do you mean, Mr. Holiday? You mean like H.K. McCard's arm?"

"Well, 'at's one sort o' damage, I reckin, aw-rite. H.K. won't ne'er 'cup'rate much use o' 'at arm, I heah. Shotgun pills makes a mess out'n nerves and blood veins and such. But I'm tawkin' 'bout soul damage, son. Th' kind 'at makes us all sinners, lost wi'out hope. But 'ey's 'at great day comin', when Jesus hisself'll descend wi' a holler, an' we'll all see 'im. An' 'en he'll slay all 'em sinners whut don't b'lieve in 'im wi' th' sword in 'is mouf. Hit'll be a great day, aw-rite! By th' way, boy, is ye e'er been born'd 'gin?"

Travis gulped, never having been confronted with such a direct question about his beliefs. His family never went to church, though he had received numerous invitations to come to the Baptist church across from school. The most recent instance had been only a couple of days before when a couple had stopped by their house to ask them to atttend a summer revival meeting there. The man had said a big-name preacher was coming from Atlanta, and the Jackson family was cordially requested to be there. Ruth Jackson had been noncommittal, so Travis wasn't sure if they would go or not, but he felt pretty sure the answer was no.

"No, sir, not that I know of. If I have been, I missed it, I reckon."

"Ye can't miss somethin' like 'at, son. Ye'll know it fer certain. All ye got t' do is ax Jesus in, an' fum 'en on ye can roll an' shout an' amen wi' th' best o' 'em. It's like sa've on a rizen t' know ye're okay wi' God, when 'ey's s' many sinners all around ye 'bout lost as a hoot owl. Yeah, 'at's whut it is, it's a hoot t' know th' troof. Not one o' 'em funny hoots, jes' sorta sorrowful hootin' 'bout all 'em sinners whut don't know, I mean."

"My grandpa says you can't know about something like that, Mr. Holiday. He's Primitive Baptist, and he says all you can have is a hope, and that you won't know if you're one of the chosen until it's all over here. He doesn't believe we can have any choice about whether we go to Heaven or not. So if that's the case it doesn't matter what you believe anyhow. According to Papa Jackson, you can't do anything about whether you're chosen or not."

"Maybe so, maybe not, son. But if'n th' Spirit comes a-callin', I'd sho' 'nuff welcome 'im, if'n I wuz ye, an' ax Jesus right on in. If ye don't, ye's sorta unchoosin' ye'se'f, I'd say. An' if'n 'e don't come 'round, ye's purty well unchose, fer sho', seems t' me. So in a way I 'grees wi' yo' granpappy, an' in a way I dis'grees. But we won't know fer certain 'bout th' whole re'dition 'til 'at great day! Hallelujah!"

The preacher shouted the last word so loudly that it startled the boy, making him jump visibly. With such a sudden, unexpected movement he nearly cut his hand on a sharp piece of tin he had been inspecting and trying to extract from one of the piles of rubbish. He checked his palm for damage, and finding none, he got a better hold and again tugged on the slab of metal. It was finally freed, and he then loaded it into the truck bed after Homer nodded approval.

"We got invited to the Baptist revival coming up. I don't know if we're going or not, though."

"Not much o' th' Spirit 'ere, son. Sorry t' tell ye. Turned me out'n 'ere years ago, fust time I showed up. 'Ey's s' stiff ye could stack 'em fer stovewood. A feller can't e'en say one lonesome 'amen' wi'out gittin' th' boot. 'Ey's got a mean posse o' deacons t' strongarm a feller, 'ey do." After a pause Homer added, "But i's prob'ly better'n no church a-tall."

They loaded a few more items, an old chair and some more bits of scrap metal, as well as some soft drink bottles that would fetch a deposit, and then Homer tied the towering conglomeration securely onto his vehicle with some of his scavenged rope. The boy was hard-pressed to find a place to ride going home, but a piece of fender remained on one side and he was able to half stand, half sit in relative comfort there.

As they slowly traveled back, they encountered two figures up ahead, crossing the lane that wound through the woodlands. As they came closer, it became apparent that it was Dead Bird and Razz Wilson. At first it appeared they were carrying fishing poles, which would seem logical since an old power plant dam on Long Swamp Creek was not far through the woods. The property they were on belonged to the stange Hoechst family, second-generation German immigrants who were well-to-do and owned a lot of property locally.

The Hoechst family had emigrated from New York, and had established one of Georgia's biggest layer hen operations on the outskirts of Indian Park. The landfill site had been chosen because the Hoechsts already deposited mountains of chicken manure nearby, generating a stench that repelled most trespassers. The landfill road was an easement Harry Hoechst, the family patriarch, had ceded grudgingly to Indian Park after the county appropriated his land for a dumpsite. An ironclad rule for all users of the dump was that one had to remain on the road. The Wilson boys had obviously been disobeying the rules, but that wasn't unusual for them.

As they came closer, one could see that their lengthened devices were not fishing gear, but long-handled hoes of the type used for cultivation. They initially tried to hide the tools, but that proving impossible they stopped on the roadside and waited for the rumbling machine to pass. Instead of dusting on by them, Homer cut the power to idle and braked to a stop.

"Howdy, boys. I'd offer ye a ride, but we's a li'l' over on load an' a mite under on room."

"'At ain't no problem, Homer. We'd nigh ruther wawk, anyhow," said Dead Bird, eyeing Travis with suspicion. "Why ye got 'is squirt wi' ye?"

"'E ain't much fer size but 'e's pow'ful eager. Don't be crit'cizin' m' he'p, son."

"Still don't look like much he'p t' me."

"Whut ye boys doin' wi' 'em hoes?"

Dead Bird glared at the preacher and started to say something, but he cut himself short and changed his whole expression.

"We's diggin' fishbait. Goin' over t' th' dam t' try'n rassle in a mess."

"Well, good luck, if'n 'ey's any sich thang. Nothin' wrong wi' doin' some fishin', boys. Adder all, th' Lawd called a passel o' fishermen fer 'is dee-ciples."

"Yeah. We sho' 'nuff likes t' fish."

"We's got lots t' unload. Hope ye ketch a bunch, boys," said the preacher as he throttled up his machine with a loud roar. The two lifted a hand in half-hearted good-bye, and then they were lost in a cloud of swelling dust.

"Bet ol' Harry Hoechst don't know 'em boys is in 'ere," shouted

Homer, wiping the dust and sweat from his face with his handkerchief as he drove. The cooling effect of the open vehicle was most welcome in the face of the noonday sun.

"I've heard he's pretty unhappy with trespassers," noted Travis in an equally loud voice.

"Don't know why 'e's s' partic'lar. 'E's got more money'n ol' Solomon. I knowed 'nother man like 'im once. 'E had it all, stingy an' mean, 'n' 'e got t' drankin' an' gamblin' and chasin' loose women, 'n' 'e lost it all. Fack is, 'e died a porpoise. Jes' goes t' show ye, ye ain't got nothin' th' King don't give ye. An' bein' stingy wi' it ain't whut gits a feller happy. 'N' th' King kin take it back anytime 'e sees fit. But life kin be a joy if'n ye foller th' King, e'en wi' all th' pain 'n' trouble. Ye knows who's th' King, don't ye, boy?"

Over the din of the unmuffled engine, talk was difficult, and the boy pretended not to hear the question. But a sudden question popped into his mind.

"Say, Mr. Holiday, didn't you used to pray down in the old woods that burned down?"

"Sho' 'nuff, I rightly did. Who tol' ye 'at, boy? 'At's why 'em woods burned up. Ol' Hank McCard's th' cause o' all 'at. I wuz prayin' fer 'is soul, an' I axed th' Lawd t' either save 'im right now er send fire down fum heaven. An' befo' ye knowed it, th' whole woods wuz lookin' like th' ol' fiery furnace, sho' as I'm a-sittin' here. Him an' H.K.'s both lost as two 'coons in Noo Yawk City. I prayed fer H.K., too, an' I b'lieve th' Lawd sent 'im a message wi' 'at load o' bird shot. I hope 'e's hearin' th' Lawd tawkin' wi' 'is heart."

"But they said lightening caused that fire..."

The boy's voice trailed off as he said the words, which were lost in an unending chatter of the motor. He hardly said another word the rest of the way home.

CHAPTER 6

H.K. McCard was still in rehabilitation for his severely damaged right arm that long summer, but otherwise he was almost back to normal. He had resumed all his regular activities, including driving a car. He had traded to get one with a column shift, still disdaining the ease and convenience of a new-fangled automatic transmission despite his feeble limb. He quickly mastered doing minor steering with his gimpy arm, which he kept in his lap gripping the bottom of the steering wheel, while he reached over the top to change gears with his good left hand. It was a trick one had to see to believe, but H.K. quickly became extremely adept at it.

Summertime was a great season for Travis to relax, and he even made quite a bit of money doing yard work for local people, mostly old folks. He also picked and sold blackberries from the big burn behind his house, where new growth was now abundant. Thorny bushes were everywhere, and there was a rich crop of delicious fruit this year. Harvesting this sweet product required considerable labor in the Georgia heat, as well as enduring numerous scratches, staying alert for danger from stinging insects and snakes, and avoiding hordes of chiggers and ticks. He still encountered an occasional nest of wasps or hornets hidden among the bushes, but he saw no more rattlesnakes, even though he watched for them with far greater diligence than before. Despite the obstacles, Travis persisted, because there was no shortage of eager buyers for his berries.

Since he set his own schedule and didn't have to get up early, every week or two he would accompany H.K. on a combination raccoon hunting and frog gigging trip, an expedition that lasted practically all night. While frogs were legal to harvest, 'coons could only be chased and treed, but not killed, since they were out of season. One had to be careful, too, because cottonmouth water moccasins were big and plentiful along the rushing streams where they conducted this leisure activity.

"Yo' mama ain't ne'er gon' fergit I wuz drinkin' 'at day we wuz bird huntin'," said H.K. as they pulled out of the Jackson yard. "She makes me promise like I wuz th' Pope 'at I won't drink ev'ry time we go off."

"Do you blame her, H.K.?"

"Well, no, I can't rightly say I do," said H.K. as he reached over the steering wheel and shifted gears. "But 'ey ain't no guns 'volved in 'is 'ere kind o' 'coon huntin', so I don't fer th' life o' me see whut a li'l' nip would hurt. If'n I do fall victim t' temptation, ye'll ne'er know it, though, s' don't worry yo'se'f none 'bout 'at, boy. We gon' pick up Papa now. 'E needs t' git out'n do somethin' fun, 'stead o' jes' pickin' blackberries an rockin' on th' porch as 'is onliest entertainin'. 'E's 'ere wi' Mama all th' time, an' 'er sick as a crippled 'coon, less'n 'e's o'er in th' burn. 'E needs a outin', sho' 'nuff. Some days I betcha 'e's 'bout lonesome as a dog at th' dump."

"Oh, Mr. McCard's going? Great! I'll climb over in the back."

"I reckin 'at might be a good idee. 'E ain't nigh limber as 'e used t' be."

Within a short time the three were on their way, heading east out of Indian Park, passing steep marble cliffs that towered above deep vertical shafts where valuable blocks of stone had been quarried for decades. Both H.K. and his father had big chews of tobacco in their cheeks, and H.K. occasionally spit out the window as he drove. Hank also spit a huge wad of juice in like manner, not realizing the window on his side was up. Travis chuckled quietly as he noted Hank's dripping dilemma, but he was powerless to help out. Long tongues of tobacco juice trickled downward and out of sight on the glass. His messy problem was satisfactorily resolved by one generous sweep of the old man's long-sleeved shirt against the pane, leaving a huge chocolate-colored smear that resembled a broad brown rainbow on the glass. That incriminating stain disappeared into the door as Hank rolled his window down without saying a word, other than a muffled one-word exclamation that the boy couldn't make out.

"Say, boy, I heered ol' Hunkie Ferby went a-missin'. Ye heered 'bout 'at?" Hank asked Travis as they drove along. Algernon Farriba, the missing teenager's actual name, was a lifelong resident of Indian Park, and was a student at the high school in Cherokee City. He had failed to return home from his job some nights earlier.

"Hooter Tinley told me about it," replied Travis, "But I don't know any details. I really don't know Hunkie all that well. He's three years older than me."

"Don't sound s' good t' me. He wuz purty cozy wi' Mutt Mayberry. Lot smarter'n Mutt, 'n' 'ey say 'e had a crush on 'at li'l' Mayberry gal. Candy's 'er name, I b'lieve," said Hank, pausing in mid-sentence to spit out the window once more, sending a fine, pungent spray into the back seat that lightly speckled everything in that direction.

"He'll probably turn up. He was in our scout troop one time, and the guys say he's pretty sharp," said Travis, wiping his face and arms with his handkerchief while leaning forward a bit and scooting more towards the center of the back seat. "I'd bet he's gone on a fishing run down the river, or maybe he's just trying to make his parents worry some about him. Hooter said they had some kind of disagreement before he disappeared."

"Hm. Might be. But if'n 'e don't turn up purty soon, I'd be worried as a chicken at th' packin' plant. Ye don't mess wi' Runt Mayberry, boy. Ner wi' 'is gals."

"Aw, Papa, don't be messin' wi' th' boy's mind," said H.K. "We's 'ere t' have us a li'l' fun. An' thinkin' 'bout somebody missin' an' bleedin' an' dyin' an' rottin' ain't no fun. Ain't 'at right, Travis?"

"Yep," said the wide-eyed boy. "Uh, let's tree a 'coon and gig some frogs."

Deeper into the mountains they drove, winding along dark blacktop roads, then careening down dirt roads of decreasing size. Darkness was fully upon them by the time they arrived at an ancient wooden bridge crossing a tumbling stream. There were bottomland cornfields on both sides of the bridge up and down the road, while tall trees in the moonlight outlined meandering stream banks in both directions. They broke out strong flashlights and noted that the sand along water's edge was littered with raccoon tracks. Two bright eyes reflected back at them from across the stream, those of a big bullfrog, which they gigged right away. H.K. slipped it into a burlap sack, where it would remain alive and fresh for the duration.

"Ol' Zell Waters owns 'is land, an' 'e says 'coons is devastatin' 'is corn. If'n we kin jes' harass 'em some, maybe 'ey'll give 'im a break. Son, I saw a big cotton-mouf moccasin jes' up ahead 'ere, so watch ye'se'f," said H.K. as he waded into the swift, chilly water. "Son, go on up an' open th' trunk an' let 'em dogs out. I don't see no mo' frawgs 'ere."

As soon as H.K's big redbone hound descended the bank, he let out a howl that could surely be heard for miles. All three dogs burst into a similar cacophany, and not too long afterward they began a rhythmic baying that signified they had found their quarry.

"Ol' Duke's a good 'un, ain't 'e? Paid twenty-five twenty dollar bills fer 'im, counted 'em right out in a feller's hand, an' 'e's worth ev'ry penny o' it," said H.K. with pride. Travis stepped into the frigid stream and came alongside the two men.

"Keerful, son," cautioned H.K. "'Ese rocks is slick as owl grease, an' lots more plentiful."

They all strained against strong current resistance, trying to wade the distance to the dogs' location. It was indeed a challenge to maintain footing on slippery rocks while fighting cascading, icy water. There was heavy vegetation on the bank, consisting of a variety of ferns and all kinds of brushy plants, interspersed with an overstory of big trees, so the creek was the preferable route to follow. The water's edge was obscured in most places, and the stiff current had significantly undercut the bank, leaving mysterious black caves that defied their feeble lights.

Out of a corner of one eye, Travis caught a movement, but before he could shift his light the form had slipped into the water. He directed his flashlight beam downward, and could see a gigantic moccasin coming directly toward him. It was impossible to move quickly without falling, so he simply froze. The snake slid on by, brushing his leg firmly and sending chills up his spine. He had heard of people being bitten by such snakes underwater, but this one had evidently missed him. He breathed a sigh of relief, and turned to try and follow the creature downstream with his flashlight. There was a ripple near an overhanging bank, but no snake could be seen.

The struggle to reach the baying dogs continued for almost thirty minutes, and when they arrived it was, as expected, a scene of pandemonium. H.K. had hardly started searching with the spotlight before he located a mama 'coon in a crotch of the tree, accompanied by three tiny youngsters, each not much bigger than a man's hand. He shined his strong beam on them so Hank and the boy could see them, while all enjoyed the spectacle.

"Want t' catch one o' 'em young-uns?" asked H.K. as he held the light steady. "Ye shinny mighty well, boy."

"Yep, mighty fine pets, 'em 'coons," said Hank. "Ye can tame 'em same as a house cat. An' I'd sho' like t' see ye shinny 'at tree. 'Course ye might have t' arm rassel ol' mama 'coon out'n one o' 'er babies. Want t' try fer one o' 'em, boy?"

"Gosh, I'd like to, but Mama would have a fit. No, let's leave them alone," said Travis, reluctantly. He would have loved to catch one of them, but he'd already tried to raise one young raccoon. Unfortunately, he had acquired that animal when it was a bit too old to completely tame. He had finally given up after suffering multiple painful bites and scratches. His mother had laid down the law forbidding any more raccoons as pets. And even though he was indeed a good climber, he didn't relish the thought of doing battle with mama 'coon for one of her kits.

"Oh, boy, ye's jes' skeered 'ey's 'nother wil'cat up 'ere," laughed H.K. "Man, Papa, 'at wuz funny, when we shinnied ol' Travis up 'at tree las' winter adder 'at 'coon, an' it warn't no 'coon a-tall, it wuz a big he-bobcat. O' all th' hissin' an' growlin' an' spittin', ye ne'er heerd th' like. An' mos' o' it wuz comin' fum Travis!"

The old man chuckled and spit again. H.K. cackled out loud as he continued to hold his light on the raccoon family.

"I didn't think it was so funny," said Travis bluntly. As he thought about it, that remembrance brought an inevitable smile to his face. There had been no harm done, just a tremendous rush of adrenaline and another adventure filed away.

They pulled off the dogs, returned to the car, and then moved to a different area. Shortly they had another great race, treed a big, argumentative male raccoon, and gigged several more frogs on sandy portions of the creek bank. And so it went, well into the night, though old Hank stopped accompanying them away from the car after the first couple of times. Thankfully, they saw no more water moccasins, and dogs and raccoons were both exceptionally cooperative. Travis arrived at the car for the last time, exhausted, wet to the waist, and highly contented. He had to wait a short time for H.K. to arrive, and noted that the man was breathing harder than usual.

They climbed aboard once more, and H.K. turned it for home. It took another hour of driving to get there, and by the time they arrived the boy was asleep in the back seat. He aroused as they stopped, raising his head to recognize his own front yard. He jerked himself awake, gathered his things, and pulled on the door handle to get out.

"Thanks, H.K. I enjoyed it again," he called through the open window to his friend. "See you tomorrow, Mr. McCard."

"Yer welcome, li'l' buddy. We'll do 'er again soon. I ain't feelin' s' well, s' I'm packing it in soon's I take Papa home."

"See you later, H.K.," he called as he opened the front door while the car was pulling away. He slept a sleep of complete exhaustion, and arose late the following morning. He stretched and yawned, put on his clothes, and walked into his mother's spacious, bright kitchen. It was a Saturday, so she had not gone to work this day.

She looked at him tentatively without saying a word, and then motioned him to sit down. He had never seen her act like that, so he complied immediately, sensing that something significant was on her mind.

"Son, I've got bad news. I've stewed all morning over how to tell you this. And I guess there's no other way except to just tell you. H.K. died last night after he dropped you off."

Travis's mouth dropped open, and for several seconds he stared at his mother in utter disbelief.

"What? Mama, you're kidding!" he said finally. "He can't be dead! I was just with him!"

"He went straight from here to the hospital in Cherokee City. His dad went with him. H.K. had a lot of chest pain while you were out last night, and Mr. McCard says it got worse and worse. He lost consciousness as they walked in the emergency room door, and he just died. The doctor says it was a massive heart attack."

"Oh, no," said the boy, almost numb with disbelief, unable to utter another word. He momentarily leaned forward and laid his head on his hands, covering his eyes, and sighed deeply. Soon he was sobbing softly, and his mother stroked his bowed, curly head gently, tenderly. It was some time before she spoke.

"No word on funeral arrangements yet, but H.K.'s family says they want you to be a pallbearer. Is that okay?"

Travis stood up and walked to a window and propped his elbows on the sill. For several minutes he stared blankly across the field behind the house, as if surveying an army of black snags that poked through dense ground vegetation on the big burn. He spoke not a word for the longest time, and his mother said no more. Ruth Jackson sat and worried deeply about the effect another unfortunate tragedy might have on her son. Finally, the boy raised himself up again and turned to her.

"Mama, I'm going to walk down to the spring."

"Okay, son, whatever you say. Don't stay too long. And think about what I asked you."

"I will. I'll be back in a while."

He descended the hill toward a hidden, crystal spring that bubbled from a jumble of rocks. It was a most peaceful place, located on part of his family rental property. The soft gurgling of the brook flowing from the spring was soothing, and he listened while he looked upward through a mature canopy of trees. The big fire had come close by here, but it hadn't reached this spot, which remained virgin and beautiful. He lay back on soft, cool grass and looked up into heaven, and soon a tear formed and ran down his cheek toward his ear. The only sound was that of flowing water and a pleasant, rustling breeze in the tall poplar trees.

"God, why did this have to happen?" he asked aloud, and then waited for a response. There being none, he repeated his question after awhile, and again it was answered with silence, except for ongoing natural sounds. He closed his eyes, and his friend's image filled his mind. All of a sudden he could see him lying in that ditch last winter, writhing and bleeding. Then the frame changed and he could see H.K. happily hunting raccoons and gigging frogs just last night. Scene after scene leaped through his mind as he lay thinking, until finally there appeared a very realistic apparition of the preacher, pointing a finger at H.K., and saying in a voice Travis thought was audible, "'E's lost as a 'coon in Noo Yawk City." The boy sat bolt upright, and looked around to see if Mr. Holiday might have walked up on him, but he could see nobody. Nobody at all.

The boy knew nothing about how to pray, except for the familiar Lord's Prayer the class said mechanically every morning at school. His family seldom so much as said grace over meals. But despite his inexperience, he prayed. He prayed for H.K.'s soul, not knowing if his prayer could change anything. He prayed for Hank McCard, too, and for their whole family. And he prayed for himself, that his uncertainties could somehow come to an end. Even before he had finished his halting, amateur prayer, it seemed that he sensed someone close by. He was convinced it was that same Presence he had felt on other occasions, and it seemed so real and so very close. He opened his eyes and looked around rather suddenly, hoping to surprise whatever visitor he might have before they could hide themselves. Once more, there was no one visible. The moment's enchantment broken, he stood up, brushed off his jeans, and headed up the steep hill toward home.

Ascending slowly out of the ravine, he felt much better, though his heart was still sick over the loss of his friend. Nothing in H.K.'s life had ever indicated any faith in anything beyond himself. There seemed precious little to recommend him to the God of the universe, when "'at great day," as the preacher called it, finally arrived. He really didn't know how to deal with such complicated, personal matters. He wondered if the preacher was right, or whether his Grandpa Jackson was right. Could one have any influence on a person's eternal destiny, or were people either intended for eternal life or eternal damnation, at the sole whims of an impersonal God? Could one truly be sure there was a God at all? He didn't know, but somehow he hoped his grandfather was wrong. If so, maybe at least Hank had a chance, even if H.K. didn't. And maybe Travis Jackson had a chance, too.

He must have looked better as he entered the house, because there was a distinct look of relief on his mother's face as she encountered him at the door. He looked her straight in the eye, and then hugged her.

"I'll be a pallbearer, Mama," he said with unusual confidence, considering the circumstances. "And Mama, I think we ought to go to revival at the Baptist church. It's next week, I think. Okay?"

"If you want, son. I don't think Sue and Bobby will like it, but we'll see. I'll call the McCards and tell them you'll be a pallbearer. They'll be glad."

"Thanks, Mama."

H.K.'s funeral was the next afternoon at the local Methodist church. A circuit preacher, the father of a boy Travis knew, would be delivering the eulogy, though the minister was hardly even acquainted with H.K. The Jackson family visited the funeral home in Cherokee City that night, and viewed the body of their friend. It was hard for Travis to believe that lifeless corpse in an unlikely coat and tie was the same person who had shared so many good times with him. He reached his hand into the casket and felt the coldness of those big, rough hands, and became resigned to the finality of the man's death.

Sleep that night was impossible, and the boy laid on his bed for hours, pondering again the terrible event that had snatched his friend into eternity. He tried with little success to pray again, but it seemed there were no answers forthcoming.

He was about to despair when he thought he heard a voice. Unsure if he were asleep or awake, he said out loud, "What did you say?"

There was no audible repeat, but words formed in his mind, something like "Be still and know who I am." He became convinced that somebody was there, but whoever it was refused to answer him again. He felt a growing peace, and eventually he drifted off into restful sleep. The next morning he remembered the incident, but he really couldn't determine if he had dreamed it or not.

The whole McCard family was bawling at the funeral, even the men—except for Hank, who was sweating enough to soak his long-sleeved shirt right down to his overalls. He had a drop or two of liquid hanging on the end of his nose, threatening precipitation, and he had to handkerchief it away. But Hank McCard didn't cry, not in the least. Overall, though, there must have seldom ever been so much wailing in one place. Travis cried quietly, too. The officiating preacher said nothing about eternal matters, only that the departed man had been a good provider, a fine sportsman, a friend to many, and that he had learned to control his alcohol habit much better since his accident last winter. He indicated that these attributes were highly commendable in the eyes of God and man, but he stopped short of making any conclusions otherwise. Homer Holiday and his wife sat near the back, and Homer ventured only one or two muffled amens at strategic points during the eulogy. Travis heard those indistinct sounds, and pondered what kind of funeral his across-the-road neighbor might have preached, had he been given the chance.

Burial was in a small country cemetery where H.K.'s grandparents were buried, a short ride from Indian Park. Travis's heart was filled with grief as he helped carry that heavy casket from a big, black hearse to the earthy grave that would be the final resting place for the remains of H.K. McCard.

Turning away from the smell of fresh dirt and fragrant flowers and sweet perfume, Travis walked slowly toward the family's white '55 Mercury, accompanied by his mother, brother, and sister. His mind was unquiet, and turmoil bubbled to the surface like molten lava as they reached the car. He needed answers to some haunting questions, and he couldn't decide whether that voice from last night had been the now-familiar Presence. It had been near and comforting, but what did it mean? Who and what was it? He just didn't know, and he was almost afraid to ask anyone. As they all loaded aboard and his mother started the car, he made a decision.

"Mama, we've got to go to that revival next week. I checked and it starts Wednesday. Please?"

"We'll go, won't we, kids?"

"Aw, Mama, do we have to? *The Lone Ranger* is on that night," complained Bobby, though his resistance seemed lower than Travis had expected.

"I think we should. Travis has been through a lot, and we need to stick together. No problem, Sue?"

"It's okay with me, Mama. But I sure do hate missing *The Lone Ranger.*"

"Then it's settled. We're going, Travis. They run all those shows again every summer, anyway. You kids can watch television some other time."

"Thanks, Mama," said Travis. He watched familiar countryside flow by, all green with grass and hardwoods, tall pines, chinaberry trees, and deep, luxuriant kudzu along the railroad right-of-way. He felt grateful that the others saw it his way.

And the revival did come, and before long it was over and gone. Four captivated Jacksons attended every night. And on the second night, under brilliant teaching from that talented preacher from Atlanta, Travis Jackson was moved to walk down the wide center aisle, followed moments later by his mother and both siblings. There the Jackson family made a fundamental change in their lives.

And a familiar, unseen Presence walked with them all the way to the altar.

CHAPTER 7

Long and bitter burn the embers of tragedy, like a lingering family feud. In such instances the young may suffer most, but immature persons also tend to be resilient and to rebound. Perhaps some are simply more able to hide negative effects. In any case, life went on for Travis Jackson, and his long, hot summer was far from over.

For a while he spent an unusual amount of time on the front porch with Hank McCard. The old man showed little outward emotion over the unexpected loss of his son, but Travis could tell that he was hurting profoundly. His speech showed it, and his demeanor had definitely changed. In some ways he was the same old Hank, but there was no doubt that he was more solemn, more studied. The boy picked up on this transformation when he first visited his friend after H.K. died. Hank's other adult children, as well as his several grandchildren, were around more for a few weeks, then their visits seemed to taper off.

The blackberries we gone for the season, but there were plenty of activities to pass the time, including a continual stream of yards to be mowed, flower beds to be weeded, scout meetings, camping out with friends, and fishing trips to various local bodies of water. One night Travis would be camping on Sharp Mountain Creek, catching catfish on trot lines and limb hooks, and next day he had to be back to town early to mow the widow Taylor's grass. On Mondays, Boy Scout meetings took precedence. One night his mother let him drive to the scout meeting in their Mercury, a distance of less than a mile. Ruth Jackson knew that such was illegal because Travis was barely fourteen years old and far too young for a driver's license, but she wanted to do something, just anything, to show her confidence in him. The trip ended in disaster on the way home when a rear door came ajar. Travis reached back to close it while rolling, and wound up nose down in the right-hand ditch. Nobody suffered any injury in the incident, but Sheriff Hoke Hatfield came calling that evening. He issued Ruth a stern warning, just short of a ticket, for letting her boy drive.

The long-awaited and oft-postponed boat project was almost completed. Hooter Tinley had pushed ahead with the work despite Travis's frequent absences from weekly building sessions. Hooter, under competent direction from his father, had finally assembled all the parts, calked all the joints with genuine tar, and pronounced the craft river-worthy. Though the trip was still in the planning stages, a journey down the Etowah River was in the offing. Launching was tentatively set near the mouth of Long Swamp Creek, and termination would be at Gober Beach Crossing, where the heavy craft could be lifted from the water and placed back on the Tinley pickup truck. There were several stretches of fast water to be negotiated, and while an aura of danger was most delicious to both boys, they also suffered some degree of trepidation over the pending trip. Don Tinley insisted that they wait until the river dropped some from recent rains before they would be allowed to make a maiden journey in their boat.

In the meantime, as they waited on the river to recede, Travis and Hooter brainstormed about making a trip somewhere else to fish and camp. It could be a group affair, something not feasible for their boat trip, in view of the small size of their newly completed craft. The boys decided to invite Bubba Bean and his cousins, Ridge and Monkey-wrench McTaggart, to spend the night with them at Long Swamp Dam. They realized that there was risk in having such a rowdy trio along, but they were an entertaining bunch and seemed a good fit for such an excursion.

Long Swamp Dam had been constructed decades earlier to provide local hydroelectric power. As coal-fired plants came on line and new rural electrification projects were instituted, the dam gradually lost its purpose and was abandoned. It had been dynamited several times by locals, mainly to kill fish for the frying pan. Despite this, it still held back a significant amount of water, and just below the frothing spillway a deep hole was a fisherman's paradise.

There was a great place to camp, away from most snakes and other vermin, atop an intact section of the original dam. There was a thick concrete parapet around its summit, and it was easy to imagine the structure as some kind of fort like the Alamo. It was roomy enough to sleep a dozen or more campers, and sometimes that many would show up. From any young person's standpoint, a trip to Long Swamp Dam was a fine adventure. Ruth Jackson helped Travis ready his gear with a mixture of resignation and reluctance. The remote location and the company of three new and somewhat unwelcome participants gave her reason for deep concern. She had consented to such a trip not only because Don Tinley had approved, but also because she hoped it would keep Travis's mind off recent events.

"Son, I sure don't like those McTaggart boys being along. They're always trouble. You know what happened last time you went off with them."

"Aw, Mama, that was just an accident. Jeeps don't usually roll into the river and wash away. And it wasn't their fault," the boy replied as he packed a quilt and a Boy Scout mess kit into his pack, along with some potatoes, oil, bacon, and eggs.

"I'm still not so sure about that. When it's just you and Hooter there's never any problem. Every time those other three go, there's major trouble," said Ruth as she assembled some more cooking necessities. "At any rate, you be careful. One more incident with them and it might be your last outing with this group."

"Hooter can be a problem, too. He calls me 'Curly-top' all the time. But he's okay except for that."

She smiled in spite of herself, and ran her fingers through the boy's ample curls as she recalled the infamous Jeep episode. Don Tinley had allowed the boys to use their family Jeep on a camping trip to a deserted house on the Etowah River. An old boat-launching ramp, rarely used anymore, was an ideal parking place, close by a tumble down dwelling in which they were to spend the night. The brake had supposedly been set, but somehow it didn't hold. The Jeep wound up in deep trouble in the river, and it took a long hike back out in utter darkness to get help. By the time a tow truck arrived, the Jeep was forty yards downstream and deeper than the seats in water. Considerable creative engineering had saved it, but it had required a major overhaul. On the trip to Long Swamp Dam this time the whole crew would be on foot.

"Well, you get that from me," said Ruth. "And I'm kind of proud of your curls, regardless of Hooter's opinion. He's probably just jealous, so don't let it bother you. But I don't want any repeats like the adventure you had that night."

Shortly the group had assembled and they were on their way. Their walk took them along the same narrow lane Travis had followed with Homer Holiday when they went to the dump, first by way of the county easement through Hoechst property, then skirting along behind the dump before plunging into a deep cut between two mountains, where rambling Long Swamp Creek flowed. Often the creek was white with marble dust from an upstream quarrying and finishing operation, but today it was much clearer than usual. Dissolved dust never seemed to hurt the fishing, anyway. Rushing rapids cascaded through a breech in the old dam, and that spot was usually productive for a patient fisherman. The five boys chanced trespassing for a few yards and dug worms at the Hoechst dumping place, where the family had deposited tons of droppings from thousands of laying hens they maintained. Red wigglers were so plentiful that their cans were full in no time at all, and they hurried back off closed property with their bait. Farther down near the dam, a small side stream was a perfect place to catch salamanders, locally known as "spring lizards," another excellent fish bait.

Spirits were high and everyone was in a good mood as they neared their destination. It was late morning, and it appeared they were going to have a fine afternoon to fish. The sky was dark blue and cloudless, while steep mountains stood guard all around in their emerald green clothing of summer vegetation. With the season's abundant rain, lush stands of ferns beneath the forest overstory were thick and prime. They couldn't wait to get their gear stowed and get baited lines in the water, so they hurried down the trail with anticipation. Up ahead there was movement, and someone was coming toward them on the ever-narrowing path.

"Runt Mayberry!" said Monkey-wrench with some degree of alarm. "Whut's 'e doin' at Long Swamp Dam? 'E don't fish!"

"'E must fish. 'E's got a whole stringer full," noted Ridge. "Le's hide...no, 'e's already seen us."

"Howdy, boys," Mayberry glowered as he approached, sounding hardly friendly. Behind him were his brother-in-law, Poss Wilson, and the two Wilson boys, Dead Bird and Razz. Each of them had at least twenty to thirty of the biggest, finest fish that could be had from Long Swamp Creek. One of them carried a makeshift net, made from a piece of green hickory sapling bent so that the two ends could be tied together, and a hundred-pound potato sack threaded onto the loop so that the burlap mouth stayed wide open. None of them carried any other fishing gear.

"Man, what a catch!" said Travis with a whistle. "Don't see how there can be any left. I hope they bite that good for us."

"'Ey will, skinny," said Razz. "If'n ye use th' right bait. 'Ey's thick as hair on a dog's back in 'ere."

"What did you use?" asked Hooter, who was bolder than the others. Runt Mayberry and the Wilsons occasionally needed help with electric things, and the only man in town who could fix them was Don Tinley. Somewhat like a town doctor, nobody wanted to be on Tinley's bad side.

"Secret recipe," said Runt, now scowling a little. "Don't ax no fisherman too many questions, I 'speck ye might fin' out somethin' ye don't wan' t' know."

"I see," said Hooter "Like a little blasting stuff? Or a crank phone?"

"Now I ain't sayin' whut we used fer bait, an' 'at's jes' 'bout 'nuff questions. Move out'n th' way. Break a leg er git snakebit, which e'er suits ye," said Runt as he brushed by them, followed by his companions in tandem. Dead Bird and Razz both shot an evil glance at Travis as they moved by, and Razz slapped him slightly with his long stringer of fish.

"Well, don't 'at beat all? I bet 'ey's not 'nother fish o' no kind in Long Swamp," said Bubba Bean as the burdened men moved out of sight. "Ye know 'ey dynamited th' pool b'low th' dam. 'At flat-out jes' down th' crick's perfect fer scoopin' 'em up."

"We ought to go tell Sheriff Hoke. He'd have the game warden on their case," said Hooter "But it's a long hike back and we're already here. Plus we've got no proof. I say we camp and try fishing anyhow."

"Good idea. I've heard old Runt might kill you for reporting something like this, too. Maybe we don't want to be that far over on his bad side. He'd know for sure who reported him," Travis added. "I certainly don't want him sniping at me. Mr. McCard says the Wilsons aren't very dangerous, but that Runt will kill you in a minute. He claims Runt actually has killed some people."

"He might come back and kill us jes' 'cause we saw 'im wi' 'em fish," fretted Bubba. "Ridge, reckin we ort t' head back home?"

"Aw, Bubba, ye's th' biggest worrier in Cherokee County. Heck, no, we ain't goin' back nowhere. We're 'ere t' camp an' fish, an' 'at's whut we're gonna do. Runt's got 'is hands full wi' too many fish t' be studdin' 'bout us."

"Maybe ye's right. But it's gonna be a long night, jes' th' same."

There was no sign of anyone else at the fishing hole. The rushing water was as picturesque as ever, and looked as if it should yield success. Travis unstrung a black silk line wound around his pole, being careful to avoid the sharp barb and point. He checked it to make certain all was in order, adjusted his red-and-white bobber to about five feet above the hook, and checked the split-shot lead sinker for security. He reached into his coffee can and chased spring lizards round and round with his hand until he caught a plump, energetic specimen. He forced the tip of his hook into the creature's mouth and pushed the fine point out to emerge just behind its front leg, missing all vital structures. The lizard writhed vigorously, in such a fashion that no fish could possibly resist such a tantalizing morsel. He walked to his lucky spot just short of the rapid water shooting through the breach, sat down, and placed his bait in exactly the right location for fishing action. Soon all five boys had their lines in the water in similar manner, but several hours of offering the most tempting baits produced no bites. Frustration inevitably began to show.

"I jes' knew it. 'Ey got 'em all. 'Ey ain't no fish a-tall in 'is creek now," said Monkey-wrench, shaking his head as he idly handled his pole. He lifted his line occasionally to assess the bait. "Else 'is worm ain't tryin' very hard."

"Looks like what we were afraid happened is just exactly what did happen," said Travis as he lifted his own line from the water again to check the squirming spring lizard. The creature looked as spry as could be, so he lowered the pole with a resigned plop, having no expectation of success. Something suddenly grabbed the line with a firm jerk, and he had a fish on! A big one!

It took several minutes of tussling, but shortly he had the fish out on the bank. It was a channel catfish, its steel blue sides glistening in the late afternoon sun, and it weighed perhaps three pounds, a fine catch on any day. On this day, it was especially welcome, because their backup food, absent a catch, was exceedingly austere. There would be plenty of fish now. Travis carefully removed the hook and anchored the fish at water's edge with a stringer, which he attached firmly to a bankside sapling.

Having no further success after some time, they all stripped down to birthday suits and took a plunge into the rushing waters. Travis knew that his mother would be horrified if she knew he was in the creek, but she didn't have to know, and it was innocent fun. They liked to jump head first off a residual rampart left over from the dam structure, and land in the deepest part of the pool. The bottom was littered with irregular concrete blocks and metal reinforcements, and an occasional intact cable, so they had to be careful not to dive deeply. Because of the copious rubble, great care was required when emerging onto the bank. They splashed around like frolicking river otters for the better part of an hour, entering and leaving the swimming hole repeatedly. To the boys it seemed as safe as a city swimming pool.

Doing just one more dive Travis felt a steely hand grab him by the leg, and he was caught several feet under the surface. The others couldn't see him, given the fast, boiling water and its tainted color. He felt panicky and struggled like a hooked fish trying to break the iron hold. Just when he was almost forced to exhale, he managed to break free, and he shot to the surface, gasping for air. Whatever had held him had cut into his foot, causing a nasty wound. He dragged himself from the water, panting like an overworked dog, trying to catch his breath.

"Wow, Curly-top, I was getting worried! Man, are you bleeding!" said Hooter, kneeling and looking at Travis's foot, which was quickly accumulating a puddle of blood where he stood.

"Ouch," said Travis. "Throw me my underwear so I can put pressure on it."

"Got t' not go too deep. Ye got into some old reinforcin' arn," said Ridge. "Happened t' me one time, too. I might nigh drownded."

Playtime was over for all of them after the incident, and the others gathered around to inspect the injury. Travis held pressure on the wound until the bleeding slowed, then finally stopped completely.

"Gonna be able to walk home, Curly-top?" Hooter asked later as they ate fish and talked around the fire at their campsite. "That looks deep."

"I think so," said Travis as he bound the foot with several band-aids he had brought along. "It's not as bad as it looks. I don't know what I'm going to tell Mama about this, though. I can't get all this blood out of my underwear, so she's pretty certain to find out about it. She's convinced that going off with you guys is what gets me into trouble."

"No way, ye make yo' own trouble. Not my fault," said Bubba. "Why's she blame us?"

"Because every time something like this happens, you guys are along. I know you can't help it, but she thinks you're responsible. And she might not let me go places with you again."

"What a worry wart mama ye got. Glad mine ain't s' picky," said Ridge. "Jes' 'cause ye cut yo' foot, ye can't go off wi' me no mo'. 'At ain't fair a-tall."

"We'll see. Maybe she won't notice," mulled Travis. "I could throw away my underwear, but it would be hard to explain what happened to them."

"Oh, she'll notice, aw-rite. Mamas notice everythin'. Don't e'en try t' hide it," advised Ridge, sounding quite proud of his elderly wisdom. "Jes' limp right in wavin' 'em bloody skivvies an' 'fess up."

"I guess that's what I'll do. I just hope I can still work next week. I'm supposed to help Harry Hoechst mow their grass and clean out their chicken houses. Big money proposition."

"Man, I'd be hoping the foot would keep me from that kind of work. Ever seen the size of those hen houses?" asked Hooter. "Every one of 'em's bigger'n ten boxcars. And what they have to haul out of there? You could fill up Indian Park gym 'bout every other day. Remember all that stuff where we dug bait? Man, what a stink!"

"Oh, sure. I know. But I can do it."

"Good luck. I'm working the store this summer, and I like that just fine."

"Say, guys, are we gonna say anything to anybody about Runt and the Wilsons?"

"Hush yo' mouth, Travis. We's eatin' fish, ain't we?" said Ridge. "Le's don't mess wi' 'at bunch."

"Probably a good idea. We don't want to come up missing, do we?"

"Ye mean like ol' Hunkie Ferby?" asked Monkey-wrench from a corner of the fort where he was lying sprawled on his quilt, full and satisfied.

"Say, you guys got any idea what happened to him?" asked Travis. "Mighty suspicious he hasn't turned up yet. A Cherokee County deputy was by our house last week asking questions. I couldn't remember anything that might help their investigation. Hunkie and I had very little contact, but I took over a scout project of his back in the spring. He's been out of the scouts for over a year, and somebody had to take up where he left off."

"Th' sheriff's been t' our house, too, and I tol' 'im Hunkie's got t' be dead," said Ridge. "He shoulda known better'n t' mess wi' Candy Mayberry. 'Course I didn't say 'at t' th' sheriff. Now 'ey got ol' Hunkie on th' Atlanta news. Imagine 'at, ol' Hunkie Ferby on th' Atlanta news."

"I wouldn't put nothin' pas' 'at Mayberry bunch. Ye heerd whut happened t' Buzzy Rawls, didn' ya?" said Bubba, reaching and spearing the last bite of fish from the pan.

"What do you mean?" asked Travis as he reclined against the concrete rampart behind his back, fully satisfied with food. "I just got a haircut from him. He seemed to be doing fine."

"Well, 'e ain't . 'E's gotta git a full engine job on 'at ol' Nash o' his," said Bubba as he chewed. "Somebody put 'bout five pounds o' sugar in 'is gas tank, an' 'at purty well paralyzed everthang in th' motor. It don't set well wi' a engine t' hafta chew up sugar an' spit it out."

"Well, what's that got to do with the Mayberrys?" asked Travis, puzzled.

"Couple days befo' 'at, ol' Mutt wuz in Buzzy's shop fer a trim. Now ol' Buzzy purty well knows whut a feller needs when 'e sets down in 'at chair o' his, er thinks 'e does, anyhow. An' ye know, he cut ol' Mutt's sideburns a sight shorter'n Mutt liked, an' Mutt raised a ruckus. An' ol' Buzzy, bein' right plain-talkin' 'bout mos' everthang, tol' 'im if'n 'e wanted 'em sideburns, 'e wuz welcome t' pick 'em up off'n th' floor. Mutt stormed out'n 'ere wi'out putting 'is money on th' table, an' fore ye knowed it, Buzzy's engine wuz ruint. Now, kin ye figger 'at out?"

"I heerd all 'bout 'at," said Ridge. "An' I'd bet big money ol' Hunkie crossed 'at bunch somehow. Made unwelcome advances at Candy, er somethin'."

"Oh, Ridge, people don't get rid of boys who come courting. Boys chasin' after girls is as natural as breathing, and even ol' Runt's got to know that. An' Mutt, too, as dumb as he is. At least I hope that's not the way it usually goes," said Hooter "It's risky enough without that."

"Risky but worth it fer th' right one," said Monkey-wrench. "Most of 'em is wall-eyed er knock-kneed er buck-toothed er dumb as a post er somethin'. But 'at Candy, she's sweet as a mouthful o' molasses an' shaped like Trixie Wills. She jes' ain't fum th' same mold as th' rest o' 'em Mayberrys. I've heered tell 'at 'er real pappy wuz a postman in

Indian Park, and 'e disappeared wi'out a trace befo' she got borned. An' she shore is purty. I hope ol' Hunkie disappeared happy. Man, I wish 'at bunch had brought 'at li'l gal 'ere t' th' dam an' fergot t' take 'er home, an 'ey could have ev'ry fish in th' county, far's I'm concerned."

"Yeah, and then you'd get yourself shot," said Hooter solemnly. "And the rest of us, too, for that matter. I've heard that same story about Candy's real father, and my dad says it's true. Nobody knows what happened to the man."

"Um," was all Monkey-wrench replied.

Travis was more than a little uncomfortable with their discussion, and he slept a bit fitfully that night, the ache in his foot adding to his restlessness. Bubba Bean sat up almost all night, waiting for Runt Mayberry to burst from nearby bushes with his .22 semi-automatic rifle blazing, an event which seemed to him highly likely, given their earlier encounter and the lonely location. Roaring of the nearby creek and deepening, engulfing darkness made such a prospect all the more terrifying, and Travis snuggled deep under his quilt for what minimal security it offered.

They all agreed that it was best to take Ridge's advice and keep quiet. Nobody wanted an enraged Runt Mayberry gunning for him. But Travis knew he couldn't keep the illegal fishing a complete secret. He planned to run it by Hank McCard at his earliest convenience.

CHAPTER 8

It was an unusually hot day in the northern Georgia mountains, with the temperature hovering near one hundred degrees. Travis was only in his second day of work on the Hoechst place, and already his arms ached. His injured foot was healing rapidly and well, and since his cut was on top of it he was now hardly handicapped by it. He had finished mowing three acres of lawn the day before, using only a power push mower. The work greatly delighted old Harry Hoechst, who had been unable to cut over the entire expanse in one day anytime before. Now Travis was engaged in cleaning out one of their massive laying hen houses, assisted by Hoechst's son Dieter.

The Hoechst place had once been the premiere mansion of Indian Park. A Confederate hero of the War Between the States had built the house in the late 19th century. Six massive wooden columns supported a broad front porch, each towering and white in finest Southern tradition. Paint on the columns, like that elsewhere on the property, was now faded, and there were large, conspicuous cracks everywhere. Hard chunks of paint littered the ground adjacent to the house as well as the wooden veranda around the columns. A permanent colony of bees lived and thrived in one column, and honey dripped inexorably, forming a sticky puddle at its base.

Grounds of the estate had obviously been immaculate at one time, with magnolias, sprawling oaks, enormous cedar trees, and now-neglected flowerbeds in strategic locations all across the large acreage. Travis had not attempted major renovation of the yard, but had simply pushed his dad's mower to all areas needing a trim. There was much more to do, such as pulling weeds, trimming overgrown shrubbery, and doing any of a hundred other long-neglected tasks in the big yard. Despite this, the place looked significantly better than when he had started his engine early the day before.

Now facing him was an unending stretch of "chicken dirt," as Dieter referred to a virtual Mount Everest of chicken droppings underneath each long row of laying hens. The egg-producers lived in small cages, each with only a small inclined space in which to subsist, though they had constant access to plentiful food and water. The arrangement was such that any egg laid would roll softly down the incline to stop just outside the cage. A clothespin affixed to the cage was moved a notch each time an egg was collected, giving due credit to that cage's inhabitant. Woe to any hen whose clothespin failed to move at least several times during the week, because a buyer from a grocery store chain came around regularly to purchase fat laying hens that had passed their prime in egg production.

All cages were joined together so that egg collection could be accomplished easily by simply walking down each row of chickens pushing a gathering cart. There were eight parallel rows that stretched from one end of the structure to the other, and two thousand cages were on line in the main house. Each egg had to be collected and the appropriate clothespin moved, then it was on to the next cage. When the cart was full, it had to be rolled by hand to the main house, where every egg was subjected to a special candling test that identified any faulty eggs by light transmission characteristics. This was the job of Betty Hoechst, Harry's wife.

Hoechst's egg operation was one of the best of the time, and produced over a hundred dozen eggs per day. Since the process generated such a mighty amount of chicken droppings, there was a constant need to remove and dispose of this refuse. This task was far more pressing than attending any of the old mansion's neglected physical facilities. This so-called "chicken dirt" constituted the main ingredient of Travis's continuing summer job. He and Dieter were expected to dig out that awful accumulation by hand, load it into a wheelbarrow, and then cart it to a waiting truck for disposal on the back of Hoechst's property. It really wasn't so bad, because with exposure the initial burn in one's nose inevitably subsided to a point that it was hardly noticeable.

"Scoop deeper, Travis," said Dieter as they worked side-by-side, his high-pitched voice and prominent New Yorkish twang coming across clearly. Dieter was already in high school, and would graduate after another year if all went as planned. He was polite to a fault, and took a lot of criticism from his peers for his strange accent and his gushing, overdone manners. "If you don't, we'll be back here next week doing the same thing again. The sooner we get off the wrong end of these shovels, the better."

"Coming back's no problem for me, Dieter. I need the job. But I'll try to get deeper, like you say. I didn't know a shovel had a wrong end, by the way. You want a trench underneath every row of cages?"

"Yes, of course. Father likes the receiving pit to be at least two feet deep. You can tell when you reach bottom by the soil consistency. Chicken dirt is soft and moist, whereas regular red clay is hard like stone."

"I don't think I'm down to rock yet," said Travis as he lifted a heavy scoop of the noxious material into his wheelbarrow. "Smells like that stuff my mama cleans with—ammonia or something like that."

"Chicken dirt has chicken urine mixed in it, and of course your nose can detect ammonia. And it's highly lethal," replied Dieter with a grin, straining with his own shovel-full of stinky stuff. "Only kidding, of course. It smells badly but it's eminently harmless. When we finish this row, let's go have a Pepsi and take a few minutes of break on the veranda."

"Sounds good to me," said Travis, wiping sweat from his brow and face. Moisture cascaded from everywhere in small rivulets, and his shirt was thoroughly wet. The pair worked feverishly to accomplish the task, row's end in sight but devilishly resistant to their efforts to reach it. After what seemed an eternity, they finally loaded the last wheelbarrow, deposited its burden into the waiting dump truck, and left their tools standing by the henhouse door while they took a much-needed rest.

They walked across the spacious back yard, heading for the Hoechst kitchen that was just inside the back door. Pigs were all over the back pasture, and Dieter stopped to pet a big boar that rubbed against the fence as they passed nearby. The creature seemed as friendly as a puppy, and one could tell that the pat on the head was most appreciated.

"Old Sure-shot is a mighty fine porker. He's sired over a hundred little pigs since we've had him."

"Big old hog. Does he bite?"

"Only if you get in the pen with him. Tame as can be while you're out of reach. He's crafty mean, if you know what I mean."

Travis looked the big pig in the eye, but was hesitant to lay a hand on him. It seemed to him that the old boar was grinding its teeth, just waiting for a chance to light into something soft and tender. Like a fellow's hand.

Ahead of them was the goat pen, and an acrid aroma from the animals threatened to overwhelm anyone whose senses had not been conditioned, or at least dulled. The ground in their enclosure was completely devoid of vegetation, and deep erosion scars were evident among scattered, sparse trees. Even the nearby ground outside the pen was heavily grazed by the voracious animals, which could reach through the wire for more than a foot to nip away any greenery that emerged.

"Why do you have all these goats?"

"Mother likes them. Let's go pet them."

One aggressive goat, obviously the breeding male, came immediately to them and begged for a handout. Dieter reached in his shirt pocket and produced a cigarette, which the goat took right from his hand and ate quickly with hardly a chew. When the young man tried to pet the goat, it reared up on its hind legs and did mock battle with him ramming the fence with curved horns as if highly agitated.

"Gonad Bill is a little squirrely, I'd say. He's got lots of offspring, too. All these little goats are his."

"What do you do with so many goats?"

"You would be surprised. There's a group of people down in Florida that likes to sacrifice them to some kind of god," said Dieter. "People in Indian Park buy them to barbecue sometimes, especially young ones. But as I said, mostly we keep them because Mother likes them. She needs something to keep her mind busy. We can't seem to keep her occupied enough, even with more than a thousand eggs a day to candle. It's funny—she's always behind but she always needs more things to occupy her mind."

They entered the back of the ramshackle mansion through a weathered door that sat slightly askew on its hinges. The kitchen counter was piled high with days, and perhaps weeks, of unwashed dishes, and a well-fed cat sat licking its paws next to the highest stack. Dieter reached into a cabinet and pulled down the only two clean glasses, and then entered a walk-in closet to get soft drinks. The place was piled high with various kinds of materials, but by far the most obvious were dozens of full cartons of bottled Pepsi-Colas, which Harry Hoechst bought in bulk. Dieter hadn't washed his hands since the hen house routine, but nevertheless he retrieved ice from the refrigerator freezer and filled both glasses. They carried their glasses and drink cans out the front door and took seats on the broad porch. Overgrown shrubbery bushes encroached all around, providing much-needed shade. They relaxed on peeling white wooden chairs, and sat sipping the colas and watching honey drip, drop by gummy drop, from the left-front Greek revival column. Honeybees buzzed at their labor continuously, coming and going from a hole near the top.

"When will your dad be home, Dieter?" asked Travis as they cooled and relaxed. "Does he mind if we take a break like this?"

"Father will be home in an hour or so. He's been in management long enough to realize that his workers need a break for maximum efficiency. A short respite is eminently acceptable."

"I just feel a little guilty getting paid for taking a break. But I am tired, I can tell you."

"Don't fret. Father will be quite content with what we've accomplished today."

The boys sat sipping and resting, letting their tired arms recover from hours of prolonged labor. Their conversation eventually turned to the recent fishing trip to Long Swamp Dam, and Dieter showed a surprising amount of interest.

"I've been to Long Swamp Dam, Father and I, not long after we moved here from New York. The trail leading there goes across the back of our property, near where Father dumps the chicken dirt truck. I've never been fishing, but it sounds enjoyable. Father doesn't like for me to waste my time in vain pursuits. That's his opinion of fishing."

"To me it isn't a vain pusuit. It's just plain ol' fun. We didn't have much luck fishing, but we camped and cooked. We caught one good catfish that fed all of us well enough."

Dieter thought about the idea, mulling it in his mind for the better part of minute before responding.

"I'd like to do something like that sometime. I'm pretty much tied up with our egg operation, so I don't have time for that kind of thing right now," he commented thoughtfully. After another short pause, he added, "Maybe that's something I could aspire to do after high school. No, that won't work, either. I'm applying to Georgia Tech for next fall. I don't suppose I'll have much disposable time then, either. But maybe someday."

A sudden thought flashed through Travis's mind. The Wilson boys had been trespassing on Hoechst property the day he and Mr. Holiday had gone foraging at the dump. He elected not to bring it up, because he surely didn't want to be responsible for causing trouble. Mr. Hoechst was known to have a pretty good temper, and in his mind's eye he could visualize him storming into the Wilson yard, facing a barrage of chewing tobacco spit, if not worse. And Runt Mayberry just might be around, too, carrying his .22 semi-automatic rifle. Better to keep quiet and just let that little detail lie dormant, for better or worse. Besides, his camping party had also trespassed when they dug worms on posted property. He couldn't very well tell on someone else and not confess that incident.

"Let's get on back to work. We can get part of that next row done before we quit for the day," said Dieter. "Yes, Father is going to be exceedingly keen about what we've accomplished today."

Travis wasn't exactly sure what he meant by that statement, but it sounded like Mr. Hoechst's reaction to their efforts would be favorable. Dieter drained his glass and rose to go, and Travis did the same. They walked back through the dark house, past a dusty piano in the tattered center ballroom, and on by a sagging grand staircase that spiraled a half-turn down from the second floor. As Travis glanced upward, he could see cobwebs hanging prominently from the dark ceiling. There was an ornate chandalier in the room, but neglect had left it corroded and heavy with accumulated dust. All furniture begged cleaning and polishing, and in every visible part of the house stood disorderly stacks of papers and magazines, misplaced dishes, items of clothing draped here and there, and a most pervasive state of general disarray. Travis took in the sight silently, but he was developing an increasing sense of what was required to maintain order in a household, and a growing respect for his own mother's hard work in that regard.

They stopped briefly to check a litter of piglets residing in the living room fireplace, confined to the space by an iron grate. All were pure white, with pink noses and feet, and they squealed with delight when the two boys bent over to rub the coarse hair on their backs. They crowded together as if anticipating a feeding, pushing and shoving like little pigs, naturally.

"Ol' Sure-shot will eat new piglets, and their mother rolled over on a couple in one litter and killed them. We put these in here for safe keeping," said Dieter as they petted the tiny creatures. "It takes a lot of bottle feeding to keep all of them happy. That's what Mother does on her breaks."

"I'd say she doesn't get much of a break," Travis observed, wrinkling his nose as he spoke. "Sure smells bad in here."

"Cleans up okay. We just hose it all out after the pigs are big enough to go outside. Doesn't seem long before there's more to take their place, though."

"Hm," said the boy, holding his breath until they were away from the indoor pigsty, and they moved on down into the hall. "Say, Dieter, can I use the bathroom?"

"Well, of course. Just don't let the goats out of the bathtub. Mother doesn't like them to run loose inside."

Mrs. Hoechst appeared from a side room near the back door, a dark nook where only the lights of the egg candler were on. She spent many hours each day examining each egg by hand for blood, double yolks, or any other characteristic that would render it unacceptable for general retail. The eggs that were normal and free of blood and other contaminants were sold in grocery stores, whereas defective eggs were purchased by a commercial bakery in Atlanta. Mrs. Hoechst looked haggard and pale, not surprising considering her interminable time in an unlighted room, from which she only rarely emerged. She never wore makeup, and her brown hair was always in disarray. She was as friendly as could be, though, and seemed to enjoy it when company came, even if the visitor were only a young worker boy.

Travis slipped into the bathroom, where a sliding shower door confined two very small goats. He took a much-needed moment of necessary relief, while the two youngsters bleated like he was their mother. Their cries were so insistent that he hurriedly finished his business and slipped out to join Dieter.

Before long the time had slipped past 5:00 P.M. Dieter dismissed Travis for the day, with instructions for him to return the following morning. The boy went by and visited his grandfather on his way home. The old man's house was on the narrow road between the Hoechst place and the Jackson home. He then finished the trip to his own house, passing the Wilson place by way of the road instead of using his normal shortcut through the woods. Tot was sitting and rocking on the porch in a chair that was precariously small for her generous frame. Her youngest child was playing nearby in the yard, swinging on a rope that dangled from a chinaberry tree. The woman didn't in any way acknowledge Travis's passage. None of the Wilson men were visible, which was unusual for this time of day. Just in time for the evening meal, Travis arrived home.

Summertime was the season of fresh vegetables, and the boy dearly loved them. Tonight they had fresh fried okra, green beans, corn, and black-eyed peas, along with raw green onions. The meat was fried chicken, and bread consisted of corn pone laced with "cracklins," fatty pebbles that were left over after lard was rendered from a fat hog. The boy was feeling half starved after two days of intense exertion, so he ate like he was famished.

"Mama, can I go down and see Mr. McCard for a minute?" he asked when he finished eating. "I've got some things I need to talk to him about."

"I suppose so. You aren't making yourself a pest over there, are you?"

"No, ma'am. He likes for me to come. He's really lonesome since

93

H.K. died."

"Okay, but be back in an hour. You know, we've already got one young man missing in this town, and it seems nobody can find him. I don't want you out after dark. Anyway, if you're going to work so hard again tomorrow, you need to get some rest. And be sure you ask how Mrs. McCard is doing. She hasn't been feeling well lately."

"I'll be home before dark. And I always ask him about Mrs. McCard. See you in a little while," he said, waving a hasty goodbye to his sister and brother as he slipped out the door.

The preacher was in his yard attending to the grass, which he cut with an old-fashioned non-motorized push mower. Homer took great pride in keeping the cutting blades as sharp as his straight razor, and the mechanism well oiled, so his slices through the grass were smooth, neat, and effective. He waved to Travis as he climbed the bank and started up the road toward the McCard home. The boy didn't have time to stop and talk this evening, anyway, so he was glad the preacher was busy.

Hank was in his usual position on the front porch, rocking with his legs crossed and the toe of one brogand pointed acutely skyward. He grunted quietly and motioned the boy to the swing with hardly a word. He had obviously been caught in uncharacteristic deep thought. He stared across the road at the burned-over woods for a full minute before either of them broke the silence.

"Are you okay, Mr. McCard?" asked Travis a bit timidly.

"Ain't nothin' th' matter wi' me, son. Mighty hot day. Could o' fried a sausage patty on th' sidewalk down in Indian Park."

"Mighty hot in the Hoechst henhouse, too. Been shoveling chicken dirt all day. And sweating gallons."

"Chicken dirt? Hmph! 'At ain't whut we used t' call it. An' 'ey ain' no sweat a-tall t' work like 'at. Should o' been at th' sawmill back in th' summer o' ought-three. Now 'at wuz a hot 'un. Used t' have t' go nine miles t' work back in 'em days, an' I had two ways t' get 'ere. I could wawk, OR," he paused as usual, "Or I could run. Made fifty cents a day, an' if'n I wuz a minute late, it'd show up on m' paycheck. Mighty tough times. And ye tawk 'bout hot. Man, 'ey wuz days I thought 'at ol' sun wuz gonna reach right down an' singe th' hair off'n 'is ol' world."

"I'm sure it was plenty hot back then, but to me it's hot enough in that chicken house now. 'Course I don't know anything about working at a sawmill. They've sure got a bunch of laying hens over at the Hoechst place. And a real big mess besides, when you look the place over. Ever been over there?"

"Me? Naw. Not since 'ey bought it. An' layin' hens, fer kissin' a coon dog. Ol' Hoechst needs layin' hens like a boar hog needs tits. 'E's got more money'n Solomon. Jes' got 'em to say 'e's got 'em , I reckin," said Hank, lifting his spit can to his lips. He discharged a generous portion of juice into it before wiping his mouth.

"They make mighty good money off all those eggs, Mr. McCard. But I don't think they do it for the money. Mrs. Hoechst has to have something to occupy her mind, according to their son, Dieter. They sell pigs and goats, too. It's a pretty interesting place, sometimes. But it sure smells loud. I'd really rather mow grass than work that hen house any day."

"Can't rightly say I blame ye, son. 'At ol' Hoechst is ugly as a mud fence dobbed w' grasshoppers, ain't 'e? Ain't ne'er seen 'im many times, jes' down at th' bank e'er now 'n 'en. Ain't too friendly, neither. Hardly speaks t' nobody, ne'er mind jawin' awhile," said Hank, spitting again into his cup and pausing for a moment before adding, "'At Yankee tawk o 'is jes' tickles m' gizzard."

"Mr. Hoechst's okay, I think, but he's a man of few words, I guess. Dieter talks all the time. You don't think of Yankees doing much digging and hauling chicken dirt, do you?"

"'Em? Naw, 'ey's mos'ly 'bout lordin' it over us fer losin' th' war," said the old man, pausing to spit once again. "I heered my gran'pappy say he shot a wagon load o' Yankees, but 'ey jes' kep' on a-comin'. An' 'ey's been keepin' on a-comin' e'er since. An' ye jes' mark m' word, son, ye'll live t' see th' day 'ey outnumbers us reg'lar folks 'round 'ere. Jes' mark m' word."

"I've got something to ask you, Mr. McCard. You told me Runt Mayberry was dangerous. I ran into him coming back from fishing at Long Swamp Dam last weekend. We camped on the old dam, and on the way in we met Poss and the boys with Runt, and they were carrying a half a ton of fish. We think they dynamited the spillway pool. Would they do something like that?"

"'Em? Faster'n a duck on a June bug. 'Ey'd put a 'tomic bom' in 'ere if'n 'ey had one. 'At way 'em fish'd be fried 'fo' 'ey scooped 'em up," the old man chuckled. "Don't care much fo' fish, neither. Sooner eat a piece o' mad dog 'an eat a piece o' fish. 'Specially one out'n Long Swamp Creek, whur 'ey put all 'at marble dust. Got t' stop up som'thin' in yo' innards, all 'at chalk."

"You think I ought to report them to Hoke?"

"'Im? Naw, 'e don'twant t' know 'bout nothin' like 'at. Now th' game warden, 'e might, but I kinda doubt 'at, too. 'Ey's plenty o' fish t' take a li'l' dynamitin', boy. An' ye jes' might get ye'se'f set up fer trouble w' ol' Runt," said Hank, adjusting his felt hat ever so slightly as he spit again. "An' I done tol' ye, it ain't no good t' git on th' bad side o' 'im. 'Em Wilsons I ain't never worried none 'bout—'ey's jes' a li'l' bit on th' dumb side, an' 'ey foller ol' Runt like a bunch o' hongry puppies, but 'ey ain't gonna hurt nothin', I don't b'lieve. But ol' Runt's a diff'rent pan o' grits."

"I saw the Wilson boys on the back of the Hoechst property one day when I went to the dump with Mr. Holiday. They were doing something and didn't want to talk about it. If Mr. Hoechst knew they were back there he'd call Hoke himself."

"'En let ol' Hoechst call Hoke. I'd stay out'n all 'at, son, if'n I wuz ye. I bet 'ey's workin' fer Runt or 'ey'd ne'er be trespassin'. 'Ey woudn' do 'at wi'out 'is say-so. Ain't no tellin' whut 'at bunch is up t'. Could be moonshinin'. An' I tell ye g'in, boy, ye need trouble wi' Runt Mayberry 'bout like a hog needs a side saddle."

"You're right, I'm sure. You really think they might be making whiskey on the back of the Hoechst place?"

"'Em? Naw, ain't much o' a market fer moonshine nowadays, nohow. Used to drink a li'l' nip o' th' hard stuff now 'n' ag'in myse'f, but I promised Maggie I'd drunk m' las'. Ain't had none in might nigh seven years. But I betcha 'ey's up t' no good, whute'er 'ey's doin'.'"

The boy headed down the dusty road toward home as the sun set, stepping on the feet of his long shadow as it cast far ahead of him. The preacher was still outside, working on a piece of junk on his front porch, and this time the boy paused to speak to him. The older man wore the sweat of a long day of work, but he seemed as energetic as ever.

"How you doing, Mr. Holiday?"

"Hurtin', son, hurtin'. Don't ax me how I feel, jes' ax me whur I'm hurtin'."

"Whur ye hurtin'?"

"Ever'whur. An' 'is cancer on m' lip is a-eatin' me alive. Looky here," he said as he pulled down on his lip to reveal an elevated patch of reddish-pink tissue just inside his mouth.

"Yes, sir. I see it. I'm sorry."

"Got t' take 'er t' th' doctor tomorry, too. It's jes' one thang follerin' 'nother," the preacher groaned.

"Ever pray about all your hurting, Mr. Holiday?"

"Well, do tell, out'n th' moufs o' babes. 'Course I do, son. Th' Lawd giveth an' th' Lawd taketh away. He giveth me all 'ese aches an' pains, an' I sho' do wish he'd taketh some o' 'em away. An' I've axed 'im t' do it, but it ain't accordin' t' 'is plan, I figgers. Fer me ner her."

"My grandpa says everything is predetermined. What's going to happen will happen, and what isn't supposed to happen just won't. He says he's glad I went to the Baptist church and got saved, but he's got a pretty low opinion of how much good it'll do me. He says you can't know about things like being saved and such. He says you can only have a hope, and that it's in the Bible that way. You just go down to the altar and get a mite more hope, the way he sees it. And you don't need to worry about anybody else getting saved, 'cause they either will or they won't, nothin' you can do about it."

"Son, yo' grandpappy's got a good heart, but 'e's dead wrong 'bout 'at. Ye spend a li'l' time in th' woods wi' th' Lawd, an' ye'll know whut I mean. Ye'll know whenye's right aw-rite. An' ye'll know whenye's not. Like ol' Hank, sittin' up 'ere rockin' and mournin' an' still goin' straight t' hell. Ye think 'e don't know 'e's goin' t' hell?"

"Never have asked him, come to think of it. He's a mighty good squirrel hunter, though."

"Squirrel huntin' don't get nobody in, son. If'n it did, ol' Runt Mayberry, he'd be singin' in th' front row o' th' heavenly choir. An' 'at ain't likely, th' way I sees it."

They looked up at the sound of footsteps, and Travis was surprised to see the Wilson boys walking down the road. They glowered at the boy and the preacher as they passed, but said nothing except for a muffled, begrudging greeting that exuded half-heartedness. Poss was several paces behind, huffing and puffing to keep up, and all of them moved toward home as if in a hurry. The older Wilson was completely silent, and he spit a big wad of spent tobacco into the road right in front of them.

"Mighty friendly bunch," said Travis as the Wilsons moved out of earshot. "What do you think of them, Mr. Holiday?"

"Sinners, son, sinners, an' 'ey ain't sorry fer it, neither. 'Ey's a shame an' a scandal. An' 'at goes fer all o' 'em. 'At girl 'ey got, Bonnie's 'er name, jes' got wi' child, 'ey say, an' she ain't e'en married. Ain't e'en married, 'ey say. It's a shame an' a scandal. 'At's prob'ly whur 'ey's been, tryin' to shotgun th' boy into marryin' 'er. I heerd it wuz Jabo Kellett's boy whut done it. An' if'n I know Jabo Kellett, 'ey kin pull th' trigger befo' any Kellett's gonna marry up wi' a Wilson."

"Good thing it's not Runt Mayberry's girl. I hear he'd actually pull the trigger, if need be."

The preacher turned deadly serious, put one hand on each of the boy's shoulders, and leaned toward him in unexpected fashion. He almost whispered in his ear, he was so close.

"Boy, ye git on home and le's don'te'en tawk no mo' 'bout Runt Mayberry. 'Tween me 'n' ye, ye's right, though, an' I know personally o' two people 'e's killed, an' got slam away wi' it. It's a shame an' a scandal, I tell ye, but it's th' troof. Stay 'way fum 'im, boy. He'll kill a man faster'n forked light'nin'."

Travis had never seen the preacher as intense about anything. He was forced to look straight into those solemn eyes. It was almost scary.

"Thanks, I'll take your advice," said the boy as he was released, the point driven solidly home. He bid the preacher goodnight. "See you tomorrow, Mr. Holiday."

"If'n I'm still here," said Homer, groaning and rubbing his chest over his heart. "'An' ye's more'n welcome, son."

In gathering twilight, the boy crossed the road home. He couldn't help wondering why the Wilsons and Mayberrys bothered him so much, being on Hoechst property and trespassing and all. Maybe it was because the Hoechsts were giving him such good pay for his employment, and he felt badly about someone breaking their rules. But regarding Runt Mayberry, this seemed to be a rare instance where the preacher and Hank agreed. He'd take the preacher's advice and try to forget it.

It seemed the prudent thing to do.

CHAPTER 9

"Lift, boys," said Don Tinley, as the three strained to extract a heavy wooden craft from the back of an old GMC pickup truck. The vehicle was backed onto a sandbar beside Long Swamp Creek, and just behind it swirled fast, chalky waters hurrying down the tributary.

"Gosh, this thing's heavy," said Hooter, grunting as he heaved his corner upward. Travis Jackson's scrawny frame was equally tried by the boat's dead weight, and he acquired a sticky dose of black tar on his hands during the effort. Despite a mighty struggle, they were eventually able to wrestle their burden out of the truck, and then half drag, half carry it to water's edge. An expectant air of adventure hung heavily over the affair, and both boys were energized by thoughts of many exciting prospects for their upcoming voyage.

Long Swamp Creek meandered for many miles from its source in the marble district of northern Georgia, across deserted farmlands now overgrown with second-growth hardwoods, down through a swampy midsection that had once been Long Swamp Lake, transected the crumbling remains of Long Swamp Dam, and ultimately crossed a short section of active farmland before joining the Etowah River not far from where they now stood. The two boys, armed with homemade paddles, planned to maneuver their craft along a narrow channel of that creek for a half-mile or so, and then shoot boldly into the broad Etowah. They expected to ride substantial currents for ten miles or more to Gober Beach Crossing. There the Central and Southern Railroad bridge was a prominent landmark that indicated it would be time to paddle hard to reach a slim patch of sand, where again, according to plan, the GMC would be backed up to retrieve them. It was a good strategy, conceived and sold by the boys to their parents, though not without encountering some resistance. Ruth Jackson had been especially reluctant, but she had finally concluded that Don Tinley wouldn't let his boy go if it were as unsafe as it seemed to her.

"You boys be mighty careful," counseled Don as he helped them pile supplies into the boat. "If you don't show up at Gober tomorrow, I'll have the National Guard out after you."

"Don't worry, Dad," said Hooter confidently. "Curly-top and I can both swim."

"That's not what I want to hear, son," said the older man, frowning as he spoke while bright morning sunshine glinted off an expanse of bald on top of his head. "You'd better stay in that boat, and watch out for rapids. There's a million rocks just above Gober Beach Crossing, and nobody knows what's between here and there. At least I don't."

"I told you that Ridge and Monkey-wrench McTaggart ran this section last year in a canoe. Them and Bubba Bean. It's real shallow most places, and the rapids are pretty gentle. They made Bubba walk behind the canoe most of the way, to hear them tell it."

"Well, I don't know how much credibility that account deserves," said Don. "At least we've got a river that's a little below full now, so just the same be careful. And that old house where the Jeep got away would be a great place for you to camp. I might just run in there tonight and see if you made it okay."

"Aw, Dad..."

"Oh, all right, I'll let you be. But use common sense now, hear?"

"Gee, Mr. Tinley, if my mama knew how worried you are, she wouldn't have let me come," observed Travis with a sigh. "I don't think we'll have any problems."

"Just navigate carefully," said Don as the last of the supplies was loaded. "And watch out. You already have a little leak there near the stern."

"Just a little dribble. We've got a coffee can to bail, if necessary. See you tomorrow, Dad," said the younger Tinley as they shoved off.

They pushed ahead and dodged several fallen trees in the narrow channel. Excitement and a deep sense of the unknown prevailed as they manned hardwood paddles to bite into flowing, murky water, propelling their craft along handily. Several others leaks soon joined the small original one, but none of them was really threatening. Such seepage was surprising to them, since each piece of one-by-four tongue-and-groove floor had been carefully calked with the stickiest, thickest tar one could imagine. Gunnels were constructed of two carefully curved boards of one-by-fourteen pine lumber, joined in front to form a pointed bow, and attached to a hefty two-by-fourteen timber that constituted the stern. Two seats made of stout, unforgiving wooden boards were nailed to two-by-four rests attached to the gunnels. Underneath, it seemed that there was enough tar to cover Noah's ark, but despite this plentiful pitch water oozed in sufficiently to require occasional bailing duty. The gummy calking soon had rubbed off on both boys so that they began to resemble a character from a Joel Chandler Harris tale.

"Careful on the right, Curly-top," said Hooter as they paddled with the helpful current. "I saw a moccasin drop in the water as we rounded that bend."

Travis didn't know if he had or not, Hooter being heavily prone to jesting, but just the same he went on full alert. He pushed his paddle against an overhanging limb on a big birch tree that angled precariously over the stream, its roots gradually wrenched from the bank by successive floods over many years. In another season or two it would topple into the stream, creating an impassable obstacle until more flooding moved it aside. There was no snake to be seen now, and Travis thought he heard Hooter chuckling to himself as they moved past the spot.

Up ahead the river came into view, an aggressive body of water that was wide and fast, and which looked very deep and mysterious. The creek mouth was a favorite site for local fishermen, and the shore was beaten down like someone's front yard. It was littered with empty bait boxes; colorful plastic fishing floats were lodged in every tree, and various types of cast-away cans and bottles abounded. They shoved into fast water with hardly a word, awed all over again by the prospect of two days on the mighty Etowah.

"I still can't believe you talked your dad into this," said Travis, straining to pull his end of the boat straight as an impetuous current took hold and propelled them forward. "Mama finally took his word for it, after fretting over it for weeks. All of them worry too much, I think."

"Yeah, so do I. If Monkey-wrench and Ridge can do this in an aluminum canoe, we can do it in this boat. This thing is as solid as railroad scrap iron."

"And might sink like it was made out of it," observed Travis wryly, watching yet another trickle of water beside his foot. He suppressed such thoughts and used his paddle as skillfully as his skinny arms would allow.

The first rapids were coming up fast, and a narrow tongue of fast water sliced between two huge boulders making an ominous roar. The white spray looked treacherous and Travis felt a momentary twinge of regret that they had decided to do this thing. Despite monumental effort, one massive rock seemingly reached out for them and slammed the boat sideways, then in a mighty rush they were forced to totally swap ends, which put the boys into a position facing upriver. Fortunately, the shaft of pouring water was short, and in a flat-out below it they were able to coordinate their efforts with frantic paddles and get lined out again. With some practice they were eventually able to keep centered in the fast portions, and soon they were moving right along with only occasional bobbles.

"Hey, it's only two feet deep here," said Travis, testing with his paddle as they floated a lazy, monotonous section. "Let's do a Bean and get out for a walk."

"Wear your shoes. Ridge cut his foot on a broken bottle when they did that."

"I'll be careful. Say, this is gonna be some trip!"

"Yeah, the only thing missing is a couple of girls for company. I'd sure like to take Trixie Wills downriver on a trip like this."

"Ha! She's not likely to go anywhere without Red Roper. And she sure wouldn't travel in a leaky old boat like this. And get tar all over her," said Travis, wiping his hand once more on a clean part of the gunnel.

"Oh, she'd look terrific, even covered with tar. And wouldn't it be nice? To have her along, I mean?"

"I guess. But I don't think she'd like it as much as we do."

"Sure she would. This is great!" said Hooter with enthusiasm. "She'd love it! What's the matter with you, you get no sparks when you're around her?"

"Can't help but notice her, just like you. Don't think she'd come on a river trip, though. Unless maybe Red Roper was along, too. I don't think girls have much fun, anyway."

"Red Roper along? No way! Now you're takin' the fun out of my fantasy," said Hooter as they strained to center the boat for another section of rapids. Shortly they were so busy that such fanciful conversation faded.

The leaks in the boat seemed to stablilize, and bailing duties were less frequent after its dry timbers hydrated and swelled. The day became warmer, and they alternately swam, waded, and rode for several miles, enjoying a clear blue Georgia sky underlined with lush green ironwood trees and river birches along each bank. They stopped at a deep hole just below another stretch of benign rapids and fished for a couple of hours, catching enough catfish for their supper.

Up ahead they could hear, from a quarter-mile away, a most threatening sound, like the rumble of continuous distant thunder. This had to be the most treacherous fast water they would see, a section the McTaggart boys had warned them about. They parked their boat to do a walk-by on safe ground before attempting passage. Raging water fairly roared as it shot between twin boulders, spitting massive amounts of white foam, then it plunged at least a couple of feet into another dark pool below. The boulders looked far enough apart to accommodate their boat, and in any event there seemed to be no alternative. The McTaggarts had described the swift chute as negotiable, but their craft had been narrower and much lighter.

"We can do it, I think," said Hooter, "But let's secure everything first. If we get stuck, we'll just have to swim for it."

"Man, I didn't know that thing was so high," said Travis with his eyes widened. "I think this ol' river must be up some since Ridge and them came by."

"Probably. Let's tie all our stuff up, and then let's go."

They carefully placed all their provisions into a duffel, inside which everything was protected by a waterproof bag. They used stout rope they had brought to lash down their essentials, and tied their stringer of fish a little more securely to a ring screwed into the bow timber. Travis harbored considerable apprehension as they cast off from reliable mooring to the bank, his adrenaline racing as they paddled hard for the center of the river. Before they had time to consider anything else, they were caught in the grip of an unyielding swift current.

"Line 'er up, line 'er up!" shouted Hooter as the noise leve increased rapidly, and the back end drifted slightly sideways. Travis paddled madly, but he was only partially successful. The big left side boulder was coming up fast, and he instinctively leaned against it and pushed hard to try and straighten the craft. As he did so he lost his balance and toppled overboard just as they entered the churning chute.

Underneath the plunging cascade was a riot of uncontrollable turbulence, and hard, slick rocks seemed to come at him from everywhere. Travis struggled desperately to surface, his disorientation making it difficult for him to tell which direction was up. His foot scraped a slick rock as he slid through the gap, and deep beneath the falls he struck his head on yet another submerged boulder. Though a bit dazed, he fought valiantly and succeeded finally in breaking above water. He gasped for air while the stiff current carried him along helplessly. Now recovering somewhat, he looked around to see where his friend had gone.

Hooter had a worried look on his face as he sat in the upright boat, which had shot over the falls without capsizing and then had been carried by its momentum into shallow water. It was now stuck firmly on a sand bar. When he saw that Travis was okay, Hooter broke into a smile, and then into a hearty laugh.

"Man, Curly-top, you look like a drowded rat! You'll never get those curls back in place!"

"It's not funny," said Travis crossly as he swam to the shallow place, where he stood up and walked to the boat a bit unsteadily, rubbing the bruise on his head. "Why do these things always happen to me?"

"I guess you're the Bubba Bean on this trip," cackled his friend. "You look like you've got a case of the blind staggers right about now. But that's a very handsome tar mustache you've got. Makes you look a little like Clark Gable—except with wet white hair."

"I think I've got a pump-knot on my head," said Travis, still checking out the rising damage to his scalp. "But it's not bad. At least I'm not bleeding again. Man, I don't think I want to shoot that section anymore, Hooter."

"Ah, it wasn't bad. You've just got to stay in the boat, man," said Hooter, still chuckling as he spoke. "You picked a bad spot to get out and walk!"

"You can say that again. I think I'll stay on board now."

They decided to rest awhile before pushing on, so they climbed a steep, grassy bank for a better view toward where they were heading. It looked like their camping place shouldn't be too far on downriver. While they rested, they explored a little in some unfamiliar woods, where dark timber was tall and luxurious ferns grew profusely. They encountered a flowing side branch they had never seen before, one stained dark brown by some unknown contaminant. Puzzled, they followed it upstream for a couple of hundred yards.

"This is on the south side of the Hoechst place, I'll bet. This branch may be stained with chicken dirt. Mr. Hoechst has another dump for that stuff somewhere down here, I think," said Travis.

"Chicken dirt? Sure smells like something besides dirt to me. But probably you're right."

They turned around and began moving back toward their boat, dodging several deep thickets of kudzu where hidden rattlesnakes could be a definite danger. Through the thick foliage at one point, Travis could see a distinct patch of blue-colored material that looked most unnatural. He parted intervening kudzu vines carefully, and used his paddle to check for snakes as he moved toward the bit of blue buried in the vegetation. As he covered the final few feet, a gathering dread leapt from deep in his subconscious, causing him to tremble. He parted the veil of vines, and his eyes widened in horror!

"Hooter! A dead guy!"

"What? You're kidding!"

"No, I'm not. This is what we smell, not the creek!"

Hooter arrived in a flash, forgetting rattlesnakes and other vermin for a moment, and both boys stared in awe at the decomposing remains. The flesh was mostly gone, except for some dried skin on the skull, and a pair of shoes lay a short distance from the pants legs. The figure appeared to be a good-sized man dressed in jeans. The upper torso wore only a heavily stained white tee shirt, which was pock-marked with several pea-sized holes. The body lay on its back, and bared teeth grinned hideously at the boys.

"Let's get out of here," said Hooter.

"I'm with you," replied Travis. They hastily retraced their steps back to the boat, running ever more rapidly as they moved along. The closer they came to the boat, the harder they ran, as if something were chasing them. They reached their objective in stark terror, jumped in hastily, and shoved off into fast water, paddling like madmen to get away from that horrible scene.

As they moved on, the sun sank lower, casting long shadows across the moving river. The mountainous skyline began to take on a familiar appearance as they neared a place they recognized. Ahead of them was a cool, shady glen where magnificent pines towered skyward, next to where the abandoned house stood. They identified the exact location slightly late, and found themselves with a treacherous stretch of current between them and the bank. Paddling furiously, they were able to reach the abandoned boat ramp where the Jeep disaster had occurred. Both of them were arm-weary and sweating heavily, adding to dampness from their repeated trips overboard. They were blotched here and there with tar from their craft as well, giving them a thoroughly tattered appearance.

"Man, that's an ugly old house," said Travis, sweeping strings of curly hair back from his eyes, then rubbing a bit of black from his hand onto the gunnel once more. "Do you think it's haunted, Hooter?"

"Heck, no. No such thing. If we hadn't had such bad luck last time we were here, I could have proved it to you."

"I don't believe in haunting, either. But there's something creepy about it. And seeing that dead guy doesn't make me feel any better about being here. Or on this river, for that matter."

"It's a creepy kind of place, but only because it's old and falling down. Ever seen an old house somebody didn't say was haunted?"

"Sure. The Hoechst place. It's haunted now with pigs and goats and bees, but nothing worse. Come on, let's get this boat out of the water."

"Pigs and goats and bees. Pigs and goats and bees. In their house? What the heck are you talking about."

"Oh, Hooter, I don't want to explain. I'll take you up there one day and let you see for yourself."

"Hmpf," said Hooter, straining to extract their heavy launch from the water. "No such thing as haunted. No way. Not even with that dead body back there. People you have to worry about are the ones still walking around. At least that's what Dad says. Say, we're going to have to call Hoke as soon as we get home."

The boys groaned as they dragged the craft up the inclined boat ramp, and shortly they had it secured to a sturdy oak tree lest their means of transport somehow escape. They surveyed the surrounding scene, finally concluding that the best place to camp was inside the hulking gray house. There was little to recommend the ground floor, since many boards had already rotted away or been eaten by termites, and active spider webs abounded. By contrast, the upstairs consisted of a fine, spacious single room with only minimal evidence of invasion by destructive pests. As the sun disappeared over distant mountains, they retrieved their supplies from the boat, including a couple of quilts on which they would sleep, and prepared to spend the night. They would sleep upstairs, but they would cook and eat in an open area in front of the old house.

Supper promised to be excellent, and they anticipated eating well as light gradually faded into night. Hot coals were soon packed around potatoes wrapped in tinfoil, and bread was warming on a strategically placed stone by the fire. Hot grease crackled in the frying pan, and their catch of the day was cooking briskly. Fried catfish went down well with baked potatoes and bread, and soon both of them were stuffed and feeling just a little bit sleepy, yet there was still a pile of food. Embers of their open-air fire were dying, conversation was fading to an occasional word, and an eerie blackness had already engulfed them as the fullness of night descended.

Suddenly, the whole fire pit exploded with a loud boom! The blast showered both the boys with flaming embers and sent both of them scurrying, terrified, into nearby bushes.

"Git up, ye chicken varmi'ts. whutcha doin' at m' house, anyhow?" came a loud, threatening voice from the shadows.

Travis was once more trembling all over, the lingering dampness of his clothes, unsettling events of the day, and this frightful, unexpected encounter combining in a most unnerving manner. Another shot from the unknown assailant's gun again rained the entire area with red and orange sparks, several of them igniting the abundant pine straw and creating minor blazes.

"Come on out, now, 'fo' I hafta start shootin' 'roun' in th' brush," warned the sinister voice. "I don't bad want t' hurt nobody, but if'n I hafta I will. Git on out heah, now, ye heah me?"

"Who are you?" asked Hooter, his voice mirroring the same fright that Travis felt. "We're just camping! And we didn't know anybody owned this place."

"Ne'er mind who I is. Jes' step out an' maybe nobody gits hurt."

"We're coming! Don't shoot, please," said Travis. "Hooter, I'm going to stand up and walk out!"

"I'm with you! Whoever you are, here we come!"

A hearty, boyish laugh greeted Travis and Hooter as they emerged shivering from the brush. A man-sized lad brandishing a shotgun stood confronting them, creating a gigantic silhouette in front of their fire. It was evident to both of them who it was immediately.

"Mutt Mayberry, what the heck are you doing shooting up our campfire?" asked Hooter, almost threatening in his tone of voice. "You could have killed us!"

"I jes' might 'ave, if'n ye hadn't been 'ere, Junior. 'At skinny kid wi' ye ain't worth wastin' a load o' buckshot on, though."

"Travis is all right, Mutt. What are you saying, this place is yours? This is part of Darby timber, I think, just west of the Hoechst place. And old man Darby doesn't care if we camp here. Dad said so."

"'At so, huh? Jes' maybe yo' ol' man jes' thanks 'e knows everthang 'ey is t' know. Pappy tol' me t' keep all trespassers out'n 'ere. An'ye's both trespassin'."

"You shoot one of us and you'll wind up behind bars, Mutt. You put that gun down and sit down here and eat some catfish."

"Hmph," said Mutt defiantly. He looked at the golden brown plate of fish, and picked one up by the tail. As he inspected it casually with his shotgun now relaxed under his arm, his demeanor changed ever so slowly. "Catfish, huh? Got 'em out'n th' river? Might take ye up on 'at part."

"Some of the best channel cats you ever tasted. Now unload that scattergun and lean it up on that tree, and let's pretend we're friends, even if it don't hold up past tonight," said Hooter.

"Hm-m. Maybe. 'At catfish do look mighty good."

"We won't tell your pappy nothing about being here," said Hooter, motioning Mutt toward a prime seat near the fire. "Here's a clean plate. Help yourself."

"Eatin' wi' a couple o' smarty-pants whut done grad-ee-ated fum Indian Park School. Okay, I kin do 'at. Jes' don't ye ne'er tell nobody, ye heah?"

Mutt hastily devoured several catfish, along with the rest of the leftover trimmings, smacking like a hound dog in the process. While he cleaned up the last scrap of food, both boys watched his feeding frenzy in amazement. The thought crossed Travis's mind to mention the body just upstream, but somehow it didn't seem to be a good idea. Hooter likewise said nothing about it. They'd wait and notify the sheriff tomorrow, first thing after getting to Gober Beach Crossing.

"Mutt, mind telling us why your pappy is so determined to keep this part of Darby timber to himself? Is it for the squirrel hunting here?" asked Travis. "We aren't here to do any harm, you know."

"None o' yo' business, squirt," the strapping youth replied in an angry tone as he polished off the last of their oatmeal cookies. "Pappy jes' tells me whut t' do, an' I do it, no questions axed. An' I don't wan' t' hear none fum th likes o' ye, neither."

Travis decided it was best to let his friend do all the talking, so he sat quietly and said little.

"Sounds to me like you don't know why you're guarding it," said Hooter. "I'd have a hard time staying up all night guarding when I didn't know what I was guarding."

"Who's guardin' 'is place, me er you? I ne'er said I didn't know whut I wuz guardin', I jes' said I does whut Pappy tells me. An' it's none o' yo' business, nohow, li'l' Mister Tinley."

"Well, to tell you the truth, we don't have much choice but to stay here tonight," said Hooter. "Town is a mighty long walk from here, and we've got a boat we floated down from Long Swamp. We're headed out for Gober tomorrow. But we'll be out of here at first light. Why don't you stay with us here, and then you can tell your pappy about running us off in the morning?"

Mutt was deep in thought for a moment, then his eyes lit up. The idea sounded good to him. They had an extra quilt he could use, and they offered it to him. He accepted only a bit reluctantly.

"'Ey tell me 'is ol' house is haunted. An' b' th' wust kind o' hant. One wi' white robes an' long hair an' a face white as a ghost. An' a mouf full o' sharp teef 'at'll bite right through a feller. I'll sho' 'nuff keep m' shotgun handy, I tell ye 'at."

"If what you say is true, that shotgun will do no good at all. But keep it handy, anyway," said Hooter, shuddering a little as he remembered the awful sight in they had seen in the kudzu patch. "Just be careful where you point it. It might not work on a hant, but it'll sure put holes in real flesh."

Travis was a little nervous about his oft-threatening adversary sleeping in the same room with him, but there was at least a small degree of comfort in the situation. At least nobody else should bother them, considering the Mayberry lad's brash manner and the presence of his shotgun. Don Tinley had forbidden the boys to take a firearm on this outing, though they had petitioned him for the privilege. Now at least they had a little firepower, just in case. Still, neither boy was certain it was a good tradeoff, having a gun in the group, since it was under Mutt's control.

They settled in not too long after dark, intending to get an early start at daylight as promised. Before a half hour had passed, Hooter and Mutt were breathing deeply and regularly, but Travis couldn't drift off, being a very light sleeper. He kept thinking of that dead body a short distance upriver, and wondering whether the individual had been murdered. He considered endlessly the strong tensions that existed between him and some of his neighbors, including the guy asleep in the corner. He had a vague headache from his earlier contact with the boulder, as well. It felt like he had lain there for hours, while a cooling breeze drifted in through a broken window. Perhaps he would never be able to get any sleep on the rough wooden floor.

The rising moon was slightly less than full, but its brilliant light severely hindered him in his efforts to rest. He did eventually drift off into shallow, fitful sleep, sometimes half-awake, sometimes experiencing fleeting periods of unconsciousness. He found himself dreaming, fighting to emerge from deep water, struggling against an unseen enemy that seemed determined to keep him from surfacing. In the midst of his thrashing about he suddenly sat up, not certain if he were awake or asleep. His head was pounding, and he was inexplicably short of breath. He rubbed the swollen bruise that protruded through his curly locks, while breathing hard for several seconds, catching up and trying to get oriented. He felt an overwhelming need to get to a window, a ferocious hunger for fresh air, and he quickly arose and stumbled across the room. He thought he kicked Mutt Mayberry on the way, and wondered how in the world all his commotion could fail to awaken the other two boys. He leaned out through the opening, and almost felt like floating as he drank in cool, refreshing mountain air.

Alternating light and shadows painted the open area before him, and the campfire embers had already faded completely. In the brilliant moonlight, the river could be seen clearly, trailing off into the distance. Suddenly, a streaking white object fell like a meteor out of the sky, and it landed almost dead center of the undulating expanse. The area where the gleaming object came to rest began to glow inexplicably, while white pulsations emanated from it in a manner not unlike ripples on a pond where a stone is cast. This illumination then metamorphosed rapidly, changing shapes like an image in a kaleidoscope, yet without color, other than luminous white on stark black. Ultimately the shape stabilized and the whole scene became clear. To stare at the apparition was blinding, but the boy couldn't take his eyes off such a peculiar sight.

In its final form the image looked like some kind of robe, but it glowed with such intensity as he had never seen. The remarkable piece of clothing was positioned as if someone were wearing it, but if that were so the individual was completely invisible. The garment turned to and fro, showing him every aspect with a brilliance he could only compare to that of midday sun. He should have been terrified, but instead he felt a deep sense of peace, and once more there came over him a familiar sensation of tranquility. Was it that comforting Presence he had experienced before? He could feel it now! The apparition began to fade rapidly, and suddenly it was gone.

Travis did not recall returning to his rumpled quilt, but when he awoke he discovered that he had drawn it close around his skinny body and slept the night away.

CHAPTER 10

Travis and Hooter completed their journey to Gober Beach Crossing and met Don Tinley without a hitch. However, their best efforts to downplay events of that trip were to no avail, and soundly squelched their hopes of arranging another voyage when the water was lower. There would no more river trips allowed in the rickety boat. The scary details of the boys' adventure were never told in full, but enough became common knowledge that their craft was shortly relegated to an obscure corner of the Tinley basement, never to see the light of day again.

A full-scale criminal investigation followed their report of the dead body, complete with Georgia Bureau of Investigation agents as well as local and county contingents of law enforcement. The body had numerous buckshot-sized holes in the chest, but on closer inspection these turned out to be the result of multiple .22 caliber rounds fired at close range. The lab in Atlanta wasn't long in identifying the victim as Algernon "Hunkie" Farriba, the missing Cherokee County teenager. Authorities questioned Mutt Mayberry and his father, Runt, at length, as Travis and Hooter were very quickly forced to tell about the younger Mayfield's presence just a couple of miles from where the body was discovered. There was only one bullet actually in the body, but ballistics testing on that fragment was inconclusive, and a .22 rifle produced by the Mayberrys did not match. It appeared that there was no way to link them to the crime.

Summer came and went quickly, as work and play intertwined to devour all available time. Mutt returned to school that fall, remaining in Indian Park where he would have to repeat the eighth grade. It appeared to be a no-win situation for him, being nearly twenty years old and still not completing basic elementary curriculum. Most mountain kids who hadn't progressed by that time simply dropped out and subsisted on whatever education they had already garnered. Mutt seemed to be fairly prosperous, and drove a nearly new car to school every day. He told everyone he purchased it with money he saved while he had been in the army.

The Wilson boys also were changing. Travis Jackson couldn't help but notice that both of them were now driving new pickup trucks, fresh from Graham Ford Company. Razz and Dead Bird both worked day jobs at Way Brothers Lumber Mill alongside their father, Poss, so perhaps by assuming considerable debt they had sufficient means to afford such luxury. They also seemed to dress snappier and be much more clean-cut, especially on cool fall Saturday evenings, when they went calling on girls in Cherokee City wearing their newest, fanciest clothes. It was somewhat of a paradox to see them pull away from their ramshackle dwelling in fine vehicles and first-rate attire, leaving squalor behind for an evening on the town. At least they held regular jobs now, and nobody seemed to think very much about the situation.

Fall quickly turned into winter while Travis adjusted to his new school situation at Cherokee City High. Squirrel hunts after school were practically a thing of the past now, a distant memory on which he often reflected as he rode the bus home near dark on rapidly shortening days that led to December. He and Hank and the eager dogs hunted squirrels most Saturday mornings, though, and there was still joy in the experience for all of them.

The Jackson family always processed a hog for their freezer each winter, and this year a local farmer had retained for them a well-fattened prospect. They usually paid a commercial processor to do the entire job, but last year their meat had been mostly tough and practically inedible. Ruth Jackson strongly suspected that the butcher had switched meat on them, giving them the poorer quality cuts and keeping the best for himself. She decided to give Hank a chance he had been proposing for years.

Hank was an avowed expert at rendering lard from a fat hog, and had been highly critical of the way the Jackson family meat had been mishandled the year before. He had volunteered to come to the Jackson place and help with a hog killing, which would keep their meat out of the hands of that robber butcher. Fatty leftovers called "cracklins," cooked tidbits left over from rendering lard, were a delicacy on tables in many mountain homes, and the Jackson place was no exception. Cracklins were used for a variety of cooking purposes, the most common of which was to incorporate them into corn bread, a method that gave such bread a high caloric value and a unique flavor. Ruth highly prized her cracklins, and each year looked forward to a new, fresh batch.

Hog killing was almost always done in "hog killin' weather," when the temperature was below freezing. On the first really cold Saturday in December, Ruth let Hank know that the time for lard-rendering had come. Even though Hank claimed expertise at all phases of such an operation, Ruth wisely decided to hire a young man who worked in a grocery store in town to help with the actual meat cutting. She would only let Hank render the lard and cracklins, a job to be done in their back yard. They carefully saved all fat trimmed from the pork carcass, and cut the fragments into small cubes for cooking. Hank readied a substantial fire in a makeshift circle of stones arranged behind the house.

"Stack a few more timbers on 'er, boy," said Hank as leaping flames licked skyward. "Ye gotta git 'er hot t' do th' job right."

"Yes, sir," said Travis, adding three sizable logs while bending backward to avoid contacting the hungry blaze. "Is this enough?"

"Ort t' be fer now. I speck we'll hafta put more on d'rectly. Le's let 'er burn down some, 'en we'll go t' renderin'."

The fire gradually gave way to a red-hot bed of embers, but Hank wasn't yet satisfied. He had the boy add more oak limbs, and then some more. He'd make sure the fire was plenty hot before he put on the precious fat. This would be a lard rendering to remember, he allowed over and over. They backed up to the heat to keep warm, waiting for the last addition to subside, while an icy breeze stole most of the warmth and whipped it away into the vastness of winter. That same chill wind fanned the large quantity of fuel into a red-hot inferno of glowing coals.

"'At ort t' be good. 'At ort t' be might nigh hot as 'at ol' fiery furnace. Le's put 'is pot on 'ere now."

Each of them picked up the end of a pole that went through the handle of a fully-laden twenty-five gallon washpot, and with some effort they set it gingerly on the fire. It balanced atop the radiant pile of embers, and in a matter of minutes fat was bubbling and melting quickly into a roaring boil. Almost simultaneously, black smoke began pouring from the pot. Hank developed a look of alarm, but Travis thought it was all part of the process.

"We'd bes' set 'is thang t' th' side fer a while, son. 'Em's th' darkest cracklins I e'er seed, boy."

Ruth Jackson came out to look when she sensed some distress emanating from the back yard. Disappointment filled her face when she saw the incredible mess. The whole black, syrupy stew of overdone hydrocarbons was unfit for consumption by man or beast. She bit her lip and said not a word, her gentle nature holding back what she really thought of the situation. The old man's wife was sick, and she surely didn't want to add to his troubles. After all, he was only trying to help.

"Ma'am, 'em's th' darkest cracklins I e'er seed," said Hank, scooping the blackened bits out into a waiting pan. "Yep, I've seed some dark 'uns, but 'ese beats 'em all. Darkest cracklins I e'er seed. An' th' darkest lard, too."

Ruth sighed deeply, knowing that their winter cracklin and lard supply would have to come from the grocery store. Travis sensed that something was terribly wrong, but he wasn't sure exactly what, never having done anything like this before.

"Mr. McCard, we'll take it from here. Thanks for helping," said Ruth as she started scraping out the pot. She poured some of the dark, hot liquid into waiting containers, but the smell, consistency, and color told her it was hopeless. The old man straightened up from the task and started ambling slowly and sadly away, heading toward the dirt road.

"Yep, 'em's mighty dark cracklins. Mighty dark. Darkest one's I e'er seed," he said repeatedly as he receded from view. "Darkest cracklins I e'er seed in m' life."

"Mama, can we eat these?" asked Travis.

"Son, they're ruined. I thought Mr. McCard knew what he was doing, but he either never did, or else he's forgotten. You have to do it very slowly over low heat. But it's okay. We'll make out."

The boy was confused by the incident. Hank almost always seemed to know what he was talking about, and his fallibility was on full display. He was silent as he helped his mother clean up the mess, and then he minded the fire until it burned out.

Hank told everybody who lived along the road about the Jacksons having the darkest cracklins he'd ever seen. Shortly several neighbors showed up, and they all agreed that it was a fact, they were indeed the darkest ones any of them had ever seen. Jabo Kellett was a gruff but good-hearted man, and he sympathized with the plight of both the Jacksons and poor Hank. He offered, as he watched Ruth finish cleaning out her blackened pot, to send some fresh provisions down for the family, since he'd just rendered some lard and cracklins himself and he had plenty. Ruth expressed considerable thanks.

The incident did no damage whatever to the relationship between Travis and his friend, and they continued their weekly squirrel-hunting ritual. Ruth was perhaps a little testy for a while when Hank's name came up, but she did remarkably well, and shortly she put the incident behind her. Just a little bump on the road of life, she'd say. It wasn't long before she could hardly tell of the episode without having a good chuckle.

A week later, on a somewhat warmer Saturday, Hank and Travis rendezvoused for their usual morning squirrel hunt. They headed across the burned area, walking toward the far edge, where a good population of bushy-tails persisted. Hank's dogs ran ahead of them eagerly, anticipating their usual fun outing.

"'Ey ort t' be some in 'ese ol' hickernut trees up 'ere," said Hank. "'Em trees wuz might nigh kilt b' th' fire, but only one side got burnt an' black, so 'ey's still alive. An' on down th' branch t'ward th' river, 'ey's a stand o' chinkypin trees 'ey like. By th' way, boy, how's 'em cracklins? 'At's th' darkest cracklins I e'er seed, 'em we cooked th' other week."

Travis pretended not to hear the question.

"Maybe we can get a squirrel treed right up here," said the boy. "We had one get away to the hole in that big tree last time. If only he's far enough from that particular tree."

It was only a matter of seconds before one of the dogs was barking rhythmically, in a fashion that indicated he was looking at their quarry.

"Dogs is treed!" yelled Hank as they traversed the last part of the burned area, wading through clutching briars darkened by killing frost.

"Bruno's surely treed," said Travis "But I don't hear Spot. What's the matter with him?"

"Jes' still trackin'. Bruno trees b' sight, Spot b' smell. 'E'll join in purty quick."

"Oh, yeah, I knew that. Watch out for this wash, Mr. McCard," called Travis as they descended into a broad erosion ditch. "I think he's pretty close. Now I hear Spot baying, too."

"Yep, 'at's 'im, aw-rite. An' 'ey's got 'at squirrel up one o' 'em leftover hickernut trees 'long th' edge o' Darby timber. 'At's good, ort t' be able t' see 'at varmi't in a hickernut tree, now 'at th' leaves is off."

"I just hope it's not that hollow oak."

They approached the dogs with glee, glad for early action on this new day. Shortly they had spotted their quarry by using the moving man, still man technique, whereby one of them stayed stationary while the other walked to the other side of the tree. A wily squirrel would invariably move around the trunk away from a moving hunter, exposing it to his motionless partner. It was Travis's turn to wait, and he dispatched the animal with a bullet to the head from his old single shot .22 rifle.

"Purty good shootin', son," said Hank as he took the creature from Bruno, who had grabbed it as soon as it fell. He handed the prize to Travis, who slipped it into his game bag with a look of satisfaction.

"Say, Mr. McCard, you say Darby timber starts right here? Isn't the Hoechst place a little farther over? Think they'd mind if we slipped over there and did some hunting?"

"'Em? Naw, 'ey's more likely t' shoot at us 'an let us hunt. Ol' Hoechst don't like no huntin' on 'is land. Infernal shame, too. Mighty good spot o' land 'ere. I know might nigh ev'ry ridge an' holler on it, 'cause I hunted 'ere fer years, befo' 'e bought it an' posted it."

"I know them pretty well. Maybe if I got permission?"

"Ye kin try, boy. But I'd might nigh ride a goat t' Sunday school if'n 'ey said yes. Mighty peculiar bunch. I reckin gittin' rich gits t' a feller's head."

They moved on down the property line, and got another squirrel treed a few hundred yards away in an enormous tulip poplar that towered above a grove of chinquapin trees. Hank made another perfect shot with his pump-action .22. The ancient rifle reloaded when the foregrip was manually pumped rearward, ejecting the spent cartridge and inserting another. He flipped the safety on, and the two hunters were even. That was the way they hunted, precision open-sight shooting at its very best. Seldom did a squirrel hit the ground but a tiny .22 cartridge had struck it securely in the right spot, well centered on a walnut-sized head little more than an inch in diameter.

There was a big sawdust pile nearby from an old sawmill operation, and surrounding it were immense dried stalks of pokeweed, killed by frost but still standing tall. In its mature state, the soaring weed bore deeply staining burgundy berries covering a long stem. This time of year its yellow leaves were withered and useless. The full-grown plant was reportedly deadly poison. In infant stage in early spring, however, just after emerging from winter's sleep, tender young shoots of poke weed were flavorful fare that many mountain residents savored. Cooking took away the poison from fresh sprouts, and they were especially good with cracklin' corn bread.

"Son, a feller could sho' pick a nice mess o' poke salat 'ere come Sprang. Ort t' keep 'at in mind."

"I will, Mr. McCard. Mama always wants one mess every year, and she's got to where she expects me to pick it."

As they moved onward, Hank soon developed a characteristic drop of perspiration on the end of his hooked nose, and it seemed that his step was ever less spry. On the steeper areas, Travis made it a point to walk slowly so his friend wouldn't feel like he couldn't keep up. By noon they were a couple of miles from home, and they were nearing a daily limit of bushy-tails. They finally started the long trek toward home, with dogs trailing close behind, the animals apparently sensing that fun time was almost over for this trip.

"Have you ever walked all the way from here down to the river?" asked Travis of the old man as they walked.

"I sho 'nuff have, many a time."

"How far is it?"

"'Tain't fur a-tall. 'Is branch 'ere runs d'rectly into th' Eddie-waw. Purty close t' whur ye boys found ol' Hunkie full o' buckshot," said Hank.

"I thought so," said Travis thoughtfully. "But they say it wasn't buckshot that killed him, it was .22 bullets. Mr. McCard, do you think Mutt Mayberry would do something like that? Kill a man, I mean?"

"'Im? Naw, I'd be s'prised as a tick suckin' a watermelon if'n 'e did it. 'E'd be 'fraid t' decide when t' shoot somebody. Now 'at boy might git mean when 'e gets as old as 'is papa, but right now I speck 'e's purty tame."

"I hope so. He's seemed a little threatening to me more times than I can count."

"'E's like 'em Wilson boys, son. 'Ey tawk big, an 'ey'll pick on anybody 'ey kin whup easy. But 'ey got no guts t' 'em a-tall. An' neither does Mutt. If'n a Mayberry kilt 'at feller ye boys tripped o'er, it wuz mos' likely Runt an' not 'is boy."

"Hm-m. I hope neither of them did. But for sure somebody did. By the way, you haven't mentioned Mrs. Maggie today. How is she now?"

"Sicker'n a gut-shot 'coon. Can't e'en cook no mo'. I'd might nigh starve if'n it warn't fer Gracie. An' 'at ol' preacher whut lives 'crost th' road fum ye, 'e brought down some vittles a day er two ago. Got t' give 'im credit, 'at's more'n most o' m' other neighbors e'er done."

Travis nodded, and they continued walking. Gracie was the McCard daughter who lived next door to the elderly couple. Maggie McCard was dying of cancer, and the entire community was aware of her plight. Hank seemed to be in denial most of the time and often simply shook his head at such inquiries. His step was slowing ever more as they approached his house, but the dogs rallied around him, licking his hand and rubbing against his legs as if encouraging him on. His breathing was visibly labored, and he stopped often to pull out his handkerchief and wipe his brow, always blowing his nose and removing the droplet of sweat that clung persistently there. They approached a blackened tree trunk, ravaged by the forest fire, and he propped his ancient Savage .22 pump action rifle against it and sat down to take a breather.

"You okay, Mr. McCard?" asked Travis in a concerned voice. "You're pale and sweating a lot."

"Me? Naw, I'm awright. Jes' a li'l' hotter'n usual fer 'is time o' year. Son, we got us a passel o' squirrels t' tote, too."

"Let me carry yours, too. Maybe your bag is too heavy for you."

"Naw, 'at ain't necessary. I'll be fine. Le's jes' wait a minute, son, an' I'll be ready as a sawmill hand at Sunday dinner."

The boy quietly and stealthily unloaded several squirrels from Hank's bag into his own, and shortly the two of them were again making progress toward home. Before long they were walking into the McCard yard. Travis helped tie up the dogs and then went in to see Mrs. McCard for a very short time. She was up sitting in the living room, but she was pale and looking extremely frail. Having little to say to her, he soon said goodbye and went outside to help Hank clean his squirrels. After that task he ambled homeward.

His mother was preparing the evening meal, and Travis set about skinning his own squirrels so she could cook a couple of them. The rest went into the freezer alongside last summer's vegetables, a supply of cut meat, and a good contingent of other neatly packed frozen squirrels.

That night the boy had the McCards heavily on his mind. Since the family's experience at the revival last summer, Ruth had taken to reading the Bible to the kids before bed and saying a brief prayer with them. The kids seldom had much to say, but they listened intently. Tonight, the McCard situation prodded Travis to speak up.

"Mama, Mrs. McCard is sick as a gut-shot 'coon. Can we pray for her?"

"Sure we can. I'd use some other terminology if I were you, though."

"Well, she's sick, any way you say it. Mr. McCard says she can't cook. Pray for her, okay? And for Mr. McCard. Mr. Holiday says he's lost as a he-coon in heat."

"Travis! I'm surprised at you! Do you have to imitate everything anybody says? Okay, kids, let's pray for them."

CHAPTER 11

It was the last session of school before Christmas vacation, a day shortened in anticipation of the holidays, and the bus ride from Cherokee City was nearing its end. Travis sat in a window seat watching a bleak winter landscape glide by, with steep, rounded Georgia mountains in the background. He couldn't help wondering if he could find a few squirrels on the chinquapin ridge if he took a walk over that way. There was no homework pressure tonight, so he might give it a try. His father was expected home any day now from the South Atlantic's Ascension Island, where he had been working on downrange missile tests, but nobody knew exactly when he would arrive. Maybe he would even be at the house now, Travis hoped. A squirrel hunt could surely wait if his dad were home.

"Look!" someone up front shouted. "Deer!"

Sure enough, three deer were crossing the road in front of the school bus, making a mad dash for thick brush down close to a nearby branch. Travis had never before in his life seen a wild deer, but he had heard that the state game department had been releasing some in Cherokee County. Several people he knew had reported spotting one here and there. He gazed in awe at the fleet animals as they flashed white tails and quickly disappeared from view.

The rest of the trip home all the students were abuzz about such an unusual sighting. Some of the boys had known people who had hunted deer in other places, but nobody knew anybody who had actually killed one. In any event, it hardly seemed possible that a season for these rare animals could ever occur in Cherokee County. Just getting a glimpse of such a magnificent creature caused quite a stir.

To Travis's disappointment, his father had not arrived home yet when he got to their house on the dirt road. Brother Bobby and sister Sue were already there, Indian Park Elementary School having likewise dismissed early this particular day. His mother was not home from her job yet, and Bobby and Sue were engrossed in a game of "Sorry," an intense board game that usually ended with a strong disagreement.

"We're almost done and I'm winning," said Sue mischievously, chuckling as she spoke. "I always beat Bobby. Want to play, Travis?"

"Don't think so. Maybe tonight. I'm going to head over to the chinquapin ridge and see if I can get a couple of squirrels."

"She always cheats," said Bobby, his exasperation barely controlled. "Make her stop, Travis."

"I'm not the boss around here. You've got to fend for yourself when it comes to board games, Bobby. Oh, want to go squirrel hunting with me?"

"No. You always walk too far. And Dad's going to be home tonight, I hope."

"I hope so, too," Travis called as he headed for his room to change clothes. He slipped into an old pair of jeans, a green flannel shirt, and his brogands. He grabbed a pocketful of .22 shells, then reached into his closet for his familiar German .22 rifle. He looked briefly at his shiny .12 gauge shotgun, but quickly dismissed the thought. He wasn't going to ask Hank to make a rapid walk to the chinquapin ridge, since the old man had to take his time these days, and he was slightly tempted to take the easier, more certain weapon. But on second thought, he didn't want to shoot his quarry so full of holes, anyway. Shortly he was on his way out the door after a reluctant bout of refereeing his younger siblings on a questionable call about their game.

The late December forest had already been hunted hard, but he felt sure there would be some action where the hickory nuts and chinquapins still covered the ground in good quantities. He went down the hill behind their house, angled along one edge of the big burn on a path he knew well, and walked for almost an hour before he arrived at the place. Unfortunately, one of the Benny boys was already sitting motionless, waiting for a squirrel to appear, at the exact spot he had in mind. He would have to look elsewhere. He waved quietly to the youth, and then moved around behind him and on out of sight.

He knew the back branch that drained the chinquapin ridge dropped fairly steeply toward the river, and entered it somewhere above the old house where he and Hooter had camped. This might even be the same branch where they had found Hunkie's body, but he wasn't sure. Travis looked at his watch, noting that he had only a couple of hours of daylight left. He hurried along, getting farther from home than was comfortable, and wondering whether he was in Darby timber, which was open to public hunting, or Hoechst land, which was not. He never located a really promising place to sit and wait for his quarry to show. He was about to turn back when he spotted a towering hickory tree up ahead, and he could see a squirrel rummaging among its topmost branches. He pushed on, fully realizing that his time was rapidly running out.

He would have to try and sneak up on the squirrel, since it was already too late to sit and wait for one to emerge and feed. Time was becoming increasingly critical, and soon he would be forced to make a desperate dash back to familiar territory and home. As usually happens when one tries to stalk a squirrel, the animal spotted him and disappeared like a ghost. Disappointed, he was about to turn around and head quickly home when he noted what looked like a clearing virtually dead ahead. He eased up and parted a final barrier of brush to have a look, and sure enough, there was an open field containing several acres. Black topsoil had been recently tilled, and stray white chicken feathers drifted around lazily as a soft breeze stimulated their motion. Someone was obviously using chicken manure to fertilize this plot of land, a fact confirmed by a strong ammonia smell.

Across the way he could see no chicken houses, but an idle John Deere tractor was parked between two buildings, an old, unfamiliar Jeep stood in one shed, and beside that building was another low shack. There was no dwelling house, nor was there anybody about, as far as he could see.

He had a long ways to go and not much daylight to get there, so he turned to enter the thicket again. Before he could leave the field, though, he heard the sound of swearing, followed a stinging sensation in his left arm that occurred almost simultaneously with a loud bang. Someone was shooting at him! He instinctively dove straight ahead and plunged into the tangle headlong, losing his bearings in his fright, confusion, and disarray. As a hail of additional shots was fired, he got up and put some distance between himself and the field edge. As he scrambled, a steady crack-crack of gunfire rained bullets into overhead limbs. Terrified, he ran madly away from the threatening sound, bushes and vines and tall weeds grabbing at him as he went. At one point he slipped on a steep, leaf-covered bank, and slid down it feet first for some distance before regaining his footing. Miraculously, he held onto his own rifle, but for some reason it never occurred to him to return fire. His left arm stung, but it worked just fine, the wound apparently superficial.

Now in gathering twilight he could hear more swearing and talking and heavy footfall. He suddenly realized that whoever was chasing him was listening for the noise of his footsteps in the deep leaves, then moving toward him and firing at the same time. He stopped, deciding it was better to act like a squirrel and just disappear, so he determined to make not another sound of any kind. It was fairly apparent that his pursuers were deadly serious, and he only then remembered his own rifle. He reached into his pocket and pulled out a bullet, then slipped it silently into the firing chamber, leaving the hammer back in fire position. If they were going to get him, they'd better know he would be shooting back, even if his were only a single-shot weapon.

Agitated voices wafted across thick woods from the other side of a ravine he had crossed, and there was a lot of shouting and cursing. Since he had stopped running, they obviously couldn't get a bead on his position, and there was no more shooting. The boy was squatting, immobile, between two big poplar trees, his mind racing in abject terror.

Quite without warning, and as silent as a whisper, he thought he sensed someone nearby. A deep calm descended on him, a calm that seemed totally irrational. His impression was so real that he turned around slowly to see if anyone was behind him, but he could see no one. On twisting his head to look, he realized that just steps away was a dirt that road led—hopefully—to safety. He backed quietly, carefully, to the road, not making a sound. Once he reached it, walking was very silent on the dirt, and he quickly put some distance between himself and the unknown aggressors. Shortly he broke into a vigorous run. As he rushed along he remembered his cocked rifle, and he quietly eased the hammer into safety position.

In some nearby woods he heard an engine start, loud and menacing. It was very close by, and before he knew it a growling, smoking machine pulled toward the road, emerging from dense forest. Once more horror rose in his mind, and he was convinced that his pursuers had swiftly outsmarted him and caught up with him. He again pulled back the hammer on his rifle and turned toward the rapidly approaching light, ready to do battle if necessary. The threatening vehicle had only one headlight, which shined brightly in the quickening darkness. The boy spun and broke into a terrified sprint as the machine wheeled into the road and came nearer, putting him squarely in the light. It was useless. He couldn't outrun them. He whirled and shouldered his rifle, pointing it directly at the oncoming vehicle.

"Whoa, boy!" came a shout from the unknown driver. "I'm yo' neighbor! Put down 'at gun!"

The man killed his headlight, and there was just enough visibility for the boy to make out the hefty form of Homer Holiday. The familiar shape of the truck-tractor materialized, and the preacher stepped feistily down beside him.

"Ye sho' do look a mess, boy. Ye's all sweaty an' dirty, an' look like ol' Satan hisse'f is on yo' heels."

"Mr. Holiday! Man, am I glad to see you! What are you doing here?"

"Gittin' a load o' scrap arn off'n a ol' car. Somebody lef' a '39 Ford sittin' in 'em woods o'er 'ere. Got two might nigh new sprangs off'n 'er, and a good load o' arn fer th' scrap heap. Ort t' fetch a-plenty. An' it's a good thang, th' way th' price o' her medicine's been goin' up."

"I—I need a ride home, Mr. Holiday. I've been squirrel hunting, and I stayed too late, and I'm a little lost, I guess," said Travis as he unloaded his rifle.

"An' if'n I had m' guess, I'd say ye had a run-in wi' ol' Lucifer, too. Git on up 'ere an' le's ride."

"Gee, thanks," said the boy as he climbed aboard, finding a seat amid the rubble in the bed. Shortly they had left the frightening place far behind.

"Where are we?" Travis asked as they motored toward home. "Doesn't this road go to that old house on the river?"

"Sho' 'nuff do. 'Ey's lots o' ol' loggin' roads on 'is side o' Darby timber. Ain't ne'er e'en been up some o' 'em m'se'f."

"Anybody farm back here?"

"Naw. Nobody I know 'bout, nohow. Why?"

"There's a plowed field back there, and a tractor and a Jeep. And some people ran me off for trespassing, I guess. They even shot at me."

"Not s'prised. 'Ey's some mighty quare people in 'ese backwoods. Been shot at m'se'f a few times."

Talk was difficult over the roar of the engine, so Travis sat mostly in silence on the way home. He felt of his stung left arm, and it had hardly bled at all. There was a rip in the fabric of the shirtsleeve, but only a scratch on back of his arm.

They soon pulled into the yard of the preacher's house, and he shut down the noisy engine. As he descended from his uncomfortable seat, Travis could see bright lights in his house across the road. He breathed a silent prayer of thanks that he had escaped from whomever was the violent farmer who tended that piece of remote property.

"Mighty p'culiar sight ye is, boy. Hope ye's aw-rite."

"I'm fine, Mr. Holiday. I sure do thank you for the ride. I'd never have made it home without you. I'm lucky just to be alive, in fact."

"'At's whut neighbors is fer.ye's more'n welcome, son."

"See you later, Mr. Holiday," he called as he crossed the road, cradling his rifle in his right arm as he rubbed the back of his left arm. He entered the house through the big screened porch, letting the door slam behind him. His mother opened the door and let out a sigh of relief.

"Travis, I thought you'd gotten lost! Where have you been? You look a mess!"

"I *was* lost, Mama. Sorry. I meant to be home an hour ago."

"Come on in. There's someone here who wants to see you."

The boy entered the living room, where a handsome man with a full head of dark hair sat the easy chair with Bobby and Sue in his lap. He looked up happily as Travis entered.

"Dad!" exclaimed the boy as he rushed to the man, practically pushing the other two aside to get a big bear hug from his father.

It was really good to be back home.

CHAPTER 12

It was a dreary January Sunday afternoon, and a stray snowflake drifted here and there on winter's chill breeze. Travis's father had returned to the South Atlantic after the holiday season, and things were settling back into a routine once more. The Jackson family was watching a show on television, and all were engrossed in its interesting story line. The phone rang, loud and insistent, and Ruth reluctantly arose to answer it.

"Oh, really? Oh, I'm sorry, Gracie. Is there anything I can do? Oh, my, yes, I'll tell Travis. We're all so sorry. Thanks for calling. Okay. We'll be praying for you."

Travis heard the end of her conversation, and pulled himself away from the television, while his siblings remained immersed in their program. He went to the hallway where the telephone was located, and stuck his head through the door.

"What was that about, Mama?"

"Bad news, Travis. You know how sick Mrs. Maggie has been? Well, she died a little while ago. Gracie says she was really struggling for breath all day, and she finally passed away. I'm sorry, son."

"Oh, no!" exclaimed the boy with feeling. After a thoughtful pause, he added, "How's Mr. McCard?"

"She didn't say, but I'd bet he'll be okay. Mrs. Maggie's been sick a long time, so he's had time to prepare for this, I'd think. They're going to have the funeral day after tomorrow, so I'll just pick you up at school in time for us to go."

"Okay. Mama, I don't know if Mr. McCard will be all right or not. He never talked about Mrs. Maggie's sickness unless I asked him. I don't think he thought about it very much. He knew she was ailing, but I don't think he ever admitted to himself how serious it was."

"He's seen a lot in his life, son. He'll be okay," said Ruth, pulling on her sweater. "I'm going to walk down and see if I can do anything to help. You stay here with Sue and Bobby. Gee, it's too bad your father had to leave for Ascension Island again so soon. He's probably already back on the job there by now."

"Maybe so. I miss him already."

The boy saw his elderly friend at the McCard residence the next evening. Maggie McCard's body laid in her casket in one corner of the family living room, as was customary in the mountain community. Hank said little, but Travis could see something different in the old man's eyes, a sadness that had not been present even when H.K. had died. It was as if a part of Hank's heart had been ripped out and taken from him. He stood in one corner, looking at the frail corpse of his departed wife, blankly receiving condolences from numerous friends and relatives. He seemed not to be hearing much of what was being said, and he responded only marginally to verbal contact. Every half hour or so he would break away from his post and walk in a shuffle to the side of the open casket and just stare, murmuring something unintelligible as he gazed at his wife's remains.

Travis sensed that this was not a good time for deep conversation. He spoke some garbled condolences and moved on, avoiding looking directly into those deep-set eyes. He could tell without any effort that Hank's hurt was immense, and the boy was afraid words would only magnify his grief.

It was several days after the funeral before Travis got up enough courage to visit his elderly friend again. He had a very hard time concentrating on his schoolwork, and spent much of his time wondering what he could possibly say that might comfort and support Hank. When Travis got home from school on Thursday, he pulled together all his nerve and trudged down the dirt road to the McCard residence. It was a cold day, and naturally Hank was not on the front porch as he almost always was when weather permitted. Fortunately, he saw Gracie driving into the driveway just as he walked up, and he decided to wait and speak to her first before knocking.

"Hi, Gracie," he called as she emerged from her vehicle. "You know I can't express how sorry I am about your mama."

"We know you are, Travis. Thanks for all the support from you and your family. Dad's inside."

They entered the door and Travis followed the middle-aged woman down a narrow hallway, where there was a strong smell of smoke and musty clothes and gun oil and canning supplies and a hundred other familiar items. Hank sat in semi-darkness next to a pot-bellied stove in a rocking chair, his spit cup in one hand. He was staring at the red glow emanating from the heater, his legs crossed in characteristic fashion, with his stiff left foot pointing upward as always. He looked at Travis when he entered, lifted a hand in acknowledgement, and looked back at the stove as if in some kind of trance, never speaking a word. Gracie said a brief hello to her father, and then she left the two of them alone.

"Mr. McCard, I'm sure sorry about Mrs. Maggie," Travis began, tension making his voice unsteady.

"Is 'at a fack?" he answered. "'Course ye is, son. I know 'at. Still don't make 'is thang no feather bed, but I know ye means well."

"That I do. Sorry. Not much else to say, is there?"

There was an uncomfortable pause, and Hank finally spit in the container he was holding, wiped his mouth, and then dabbed the corner of one eye. He cleared his throat before speaking.

"I be dog if'n I don't miss 'er wusser'n I thought I would. Fifty-seven years hitched up an' I took 'er fer granted mos' o' 'at time. I shoulda tol' 'er how much she meant t' 'is ol' squirrel hunter."

"I think she knew, Mr. McCard. You told her in a thousand ways without coming right out and saying so. She knew."

"I ain't 'sputin' 'at, boy. But right now I sho' 'nuff wish I'd o' stayed out'n some o' m' devilment an' cussin' an' drinkin' an' spittin'. A li'l' bit o' sich ain't s' bad, but I might nigh made a c'reer out'n 'em. But 'em thangs ain't th' ha'f o' it. It's th' thangs I ain't done lately, an' not th' thangs I ain't done in a coon's age, 'at I'm mos'ly studdin' 'bout now."

"Such as?"

"Wal, like I said, keepin' my mouf shut 'stead o' tellin' 'er whut a good supper she cooked. Er fergettin' 'er birfday. Lawd, I still don't 'member whut wuz 'er birfday, kin ye b'lieve 'at? An' we got married in a June, but I be dog if'n I kin 'member th' 'zack day o' th' month. Naw, 'fraid I wuzn't much o' a husban' t' Maggie."

"Sure you were, Mr. McCard. Don't feel so bad. I was around here an awful lot, and I think you were a great husband. And so did Mrs. Maggie. She never told me so in straight-shooting words, but the way she talked about you, she didn't have to get mushy for me to know what she meant."

"Now, boy,ye's sayin' thangs I wan' t' hear. I hope ye ain't jes' sayin' 'em t' put a li'l' liniment on m' conscience."

"No way. You know I'd never say something like that unless it were true."

"Naw, don't reckin ye would, son. Ye's got a trooful streak wider'n th' Eddie-waw River. I jes' hope ye's right an' not jes' hoodwinked," said Hank.

He turned slightly in his chair and leaned toward a corner, where he retrieved a flat, rectangular object from the floor. Travis recognized it immediately as a picture frame, one he had never seen before, with gold trim that seemed out of place in the austere McCard home. The old man looked wistfully at the face behind the glass, his emotions showing more than the boy had ever seen before. After a long moment, he handed the picture tenderly to Travis.

The boy turned the black-and-white photograph rightside up, and there was a beautiful woman staring back at him with big eyes sparkling. Her skin was perfectly smooth and youthful, her hair glistened with health, and a faint but feisty smile was on her lips, revealing flawless white teeth. It was without question a picture of one of the most beautiful women the boy had ever seen, maybe even prettier than his own mother.

"Wow, Mr. McCard, who *is* this?" he asked "She sure is good-looking."

"'At's Maggie when she wuz young. Don't rightly know 'zackly how ol' she wuz, but 'bout twenny, I'd say. She wuz a looker, aw-rite. An' I didn't take nuthin off'n nobody when it come t' Maggie. I whupped a many 'un whut tried t' come betwixt us. We wuz happy as two fresh-fledged jaybirds in 'em days. 'Eys lots o' feed through th' chicken trough since 'en, ye kin bet. An 'is ol' barn rat sho' do miss 'er. An' I still wisht I'd a-been a whole sight mo' fer her, an' a passel less fer me. But I reckin its jes' a li'l' too late t' stoke 'at fire, son."

"Well, I certainly agree she was a sho-nuff looker, Mr. McCard. Wow!" said Travis as he handed the photo back to his friend thoughtfully. "But listen to me, Mr. McCard. You really were a good husband to her. And anyway, you'll see Mrs. Maggie in heaven, and she'll tell you that herself. You believe that, don't you?"

"Ain't no doubt Maggie's gon' be 'ere. As fer me, I'm goin' th' other d'rection. An' I kin tell ye 'ey ain't no way I kin crawfish th' right way, son."

"What do you mean? Nobody ever stops being a candidate for heaven, no matter if they do a little spittin' and cussin'. Mr. McCard, you should have heard that preacher from Atlanta last summer. All a person has to do is accept Jesus as Savior, and all that kind of thing God considers to be put as far as the east is from the west, and that's a pretty good piece."

"'Fraid ye don't know th' whole story, an' neither does 'at preacher ye tawkin' 'bout. I heered a feller preach one time, an' 'e sounded like 'e wuz 'bout t' swaller 'is tongue betwixt might nigh ev'ry word. A 'suck an' blow' preacher, 'at's whut I called 'im. An 'at so-called preacher whut lives 'crost th' road fum ye done tol' me all ye's sayin', an' I don't b'lieve a word o' it. If'n he's a preacher, th' woods is full o' 'em. Prayin' in th' woods fer m' 'ternal soul, whut a waste o' time, by Job. Ol' Lucifer'll get aholt o' m' carcass befo' it cools off, if'n I don't miss m' guess."

"He doesn't have to unless you let him. And whatever you say about Mr. Holiday, he sure lives what he believes. Not without complaint, I must say, but he still lives it."

"Ye kin say 'at again, not wi'out complaint. But ye's right, 'e ain't one o' 'em hippercritters a-tall. 'E wawks th' wawk, as 'ey sez. Trouble is, 'e can't he'p but tawk too much o' th' tawk. But I thank 'e'd shet up 'bout m' sinnin' if'n he knowed th' whole troof 'bout Hank McCard."

"What is the truth, Mr. McCard? You keep talking like you're hiding some dark secret."

"A whole chicken house full o' 'em, son. I ne'er tol' nobody befo', but seems now's as good a time as any t' come clean, an' ye's a purty clean feller t' come clean to," said Hank with a discernible sigh. He paused briefly before continuing, weighing his words in uncharacteristic fashion, staring at the stove as he continued to chew slowly on the wad of tobacco distending his cheek.

"Son, more'n a month o' Sundays ago, I wuz a moonshiner o' th' fust order. Sho' beat wawkin' t' th' sawmill an' workin' fer fifty cents a day. Did I e'er tell ye 'bout 'at? I had t' go nine miles t' work, an' I had two ways t' get 'ere, I could wawk, OR," he paused as usual and spit in his can, "or I could run. An' if'n I wuz a minute late, it'd show up on m' paycheck. 'Em wuz some hard times."

"Yes, sir, a couple of times. And you stopped working that sawmill job to do some moonshining? That was a long time ago. Don't you think God could easily forgive something that happened so long ago?"

"Wal, I reckin 'e could o'erlook th' moonshinin'. 'Twarn't much other way t' make ends meet nohow. An' if'n God gived us th' where'bouts t' make corn likker, who's th' gov'ment t' say we ortn't? An' take a li'l' nip now 'n 'gin, too. But 'at ain't th' wust part o' it, boy."

The old man paused again and took out his handkerchief, then wiped away some forming beads of perspiration from his forehead. Shortly, a droplet hung precariously from the end of his nose, and he daubed it away before blowing loudly and putting away his handkerchief. Travis sat in silence, giving him ample opportunity to continue.

"I'm gon' tell ye somethin' nobody else 'round 'ere knows, 'ceptin' Runt Mayberry. I wuz in th' illegal likker business wi' 'is pappy, way back 'ere. Runt wuzn't but maybe yo' age er younger. Fack o' th' matter is, I'm th' one whut gived ol' Runt 'is nickname o' Runt. An' 'en one day a bunch o' revenooers come in an' busted up our bes' brass still, an' I lit out like a fox wi' 'is tail afire, an' one o' 'em wuz hot on m' heels 'E didn't know I wuz carryin' a .44 pistol. I tripped an' fell o'er a bobwire fence, an' hit m' head on a split-rail post. Made a big bruisin' pump-knot on m' forrid, it did. An' jes' befo' 'at revenooer wuz goin' t grab me, m' lights cleared up, an' I whirled 'roun' an' shot 'im deader' a chestnut log. Made th' Atlanta papers, 'at revenooer gittin' shot. 'E ha a wife an' three kids, 'ey said. An' I shot 'im dead in 'is tracks. I'll ne'e fergit th' s'prise look on 'is face when I pulled 'at trigger."

"Oh, wow," said Travis, stunned. He just looked at his friend for a long minute, while Hank said nothing more, and sat simply staring at the pot-bellied stove. Neither of them spoke until the boy finally broke the uncomfortable silence.

"What did they do to you?"

"Nothin'. 'Ey ne'er caught me. Ol' Runt's pappy got caught at th' still an' did time, but 'e ne'er tol' nobody 'bout who wuz his he'per whut runned off an' whut shot 'at revenooer. Claimed he'd jes' hired 'at feller an' didn' e'en know 'is name. Runt got away, too, and 'e did'n' say nothin' 'bout me, neither. An' in th' meanwhile, I been livin' wi' 'is stinkin' deed I done, like somethin' afire in th' pit o' m' stummick, somethin' terrible 'at I jes' can't git acrost."

"Oh, wow," said Travis, shaking his head slowly.

"All 'ese years I been skeered one o' 'em Mayberrys wuz goin' t' turn me in, but 'ey ne'er have. 'Ey hated 'em revenooers 'bout as bad as anybody e'er did, an' 'ey ne'er did say nothin' yet. 'Course I always give 'em might nigh anythang 'ey wanted, 'cludin' th' pick o' chickens out'n m' chicken houses, 'cause o' 'at shadder o'er m' life. But 'ey kin have all th' chickens 'ey want, fur as I'm concerned. Druther eat a piece o' mad dog as t' eat a piece o' chicken, anyhow. I've seed 'em gather 'em up half sick an' load 'em fer th' plant, an' e'en toss in one er two might nigh dead. Foreman'd say 'ey'll make soup, toss 'em on in. If'n one o' 'em birds is s' twisted 'is bill's pointin' t'wards 'is tail, 'ey'll still crate 'em up an' ship 'em out. Nope, sooner eat a piece o' mad dog 'an eat a piece o' chicken, m'se'f. Did I e'er tell ye 'bout 'at, boy?"

"Yes, sir, you've mentioned it before. And the Mayberrys take full advantage of the situation by pilfering your chickens whenever they want?"

"Yep, sho' 'nuff do. An' I couldn' do nuthin 'bout 'at a-tall. An' when Runt's ol' man died, I thought sho' ol' Runt 'd turn me in, but s' fur 'e ain't. Don't reckin 'ey's no money in it fer rattin' on me now. I jes' might outlive th' charges yet, if'n 'e waits much longer t' tell th' tale."

"Well, I'll never tell, Mr. McCard. You know that."

"Yep, I do. Ye's a mighty good frien', boy, e'en if'n ye is skinny as a stick horse. An' a durn good shot, t' boot, I'll say."

"Thanks, Mr. McCard. You're a pretty good one yourself."

"An' 'at's th' story o' how m' worthless soul'll spend th' afterlife, in th' fires o' hell. 'At might be a tear-jerker, boy, but 'at's th' way thangs is."

"Mr. McCard, the way I understand it, you can be forgiven for any sin, no matter how bad it is. Killing somebody must be just about the worst thing you can do, but they tell me that anything wrong you do puts you squarely in hell, even little things. But Jesus offers to forgive anything, including the very worst sins. You really ought to listen to what Mr. Holiday, or somebody who knows, has to say about it."

"I've had m' fill o' preachers up t' m' eyeballs, boy. Been tired o' 'em since Buck was a calf. Mos' o' 'em jes' wants t' fill up th' platters 'ey run under yo' nose ev'ry time 'ey kin herd up a crowd. Nope, I done had a bate o' preachers an' so-called preachers. An' I don't thank mos' o' 'em care if'n a feller winds up in heaven er hell, s'long as 'e leaves 'em wi' th' plate full."

Travis felt rising frustration with Hank's persistent line of reasoning, and began feeling depressed and anxious. Just when he was practically without any more words for his friend, he suddenly thought of the burned-over woods across the road, and his conversation with Mr. Holiday.

"Mr. McCard, you know that big burn across the road? Do you know how that happened?"

"I 'speck 'at so-called preacher started it. 'E wuz over 'ere 'at night it broke out, shoutin' an' hollerin' and prob'ly drunk wi' th' blind staggers. Prob'ly lit a fire, maybe e'en had 'im a secret li'l' smoke an' dropped 'is match. All I know is 'e wuz th' only one o'er 'ere when it started. Why Hoke didn' have 'im in jail b' sunup sho' beats me."

"He was over there praying for you, Mr. McCard, and for H.K. He told me he asked God to either save your souls right then or send fire down from heaven, and before he knew it the whole woods was on fire. And he was serious. I know Mr. Holiday pretty well, and I don't think he'd ever intentionally burn anything up. He's pretty careful, too, so I don't think he'd accidentally start a fire. And I just know he'd rather die than smoke or drink. He's really got a good heart. Remember when he sent that food down for you and Mrs. Maggie? And one time I think he saved my life, sure as I'm sitting here."

"Fire fum heaven, huh? I was on m' front porch 'at night, listening to 'at ol' fool scare th' livin' daylights out'n ev'ry critter in th' woods, an' I don't 'member no fire..." The old man stopped short, and his eyes brightened as he paused and looked at the boy in a brief flash of amazement. "Boy, a fallin' star! A fallin' star streaked 'crost th' sky jes' befo' 'at fire got t' blazin'! Ain't 'at quare! I jes' now 'member'd 'at."

"Could it be that was the fire from heaven that burned up the big woods?"

"Could be. 'At ol' goat saved yo' life? How'd 'at preacher save yo' life, son?"

"Back during squirrel season I wandered a little farther than I usually do, going to do some still hunting late one evening over on the chinquapin ridge. A boy was already hunting there, so I plunged down that branch toward the river. I found a couple of storage sheds and a tractor and a Jeep, and a field freshly fertilized with chicken manure. And just when I started to leave, somebody began shooting at me. Hit me in the left arm, too, but it was just a scratch. I never told Mama about it, 'cause she might not let me go hunting again if I did, so please don't mention it to anybody. But anyhow, some guys came chasing me then, cussing and shooting like Jesse James, and I ran into Mr. Holiday. He gave me a ride out of there on his tractor. It was really a close call."

"Hm-m. 'At so? An' 'e wuz 'ere accidental-like?"

"No. He was scavenging a car close to the old river road. Oh, I don't think running into him was accidental at all. I've got this friend who protects me. I don't know his name or exactly who he is, but I can feel him whenever I get in deep trouble, and he was there that night."

"Mighty quare, boy. Mighty quare. Wal, ye jes' don't tell m' story an' I won't tell yorn. An' in th' meantime, 'ere I am lonesome as a dog at th' dump. But it sho' he'ps to have a good frien' like ye come by, I kin tell ye."

"I have to go, Mr. McCard. I've got homework. I'll come back tomorrow."

"See 'at ye do, boy. Ye eatin' any cracklin' bread 'ese days?"

"Yes, sir. Mighty good stuff with pork chops and fried okra and black-eyed peas."

"You'uns got th' darkest cracklins I e'er seed. Darkest uns I e'er seed. But I bet 'ey's good."

"Fine as frog's hair, Mr. McCard. See you tomorrow."

CHAPTER 13

Spring comes early in the South, and beautiful weekends can present as early as March. School recessed for Easter break, and the weather forecast was for temperatures in the high 70s, clear skies, and little wind. Hooter Tinley called Travis Jackson at home with a proposition.

"Hey, Curly-top, want to do a little camping trip to Sharp Mountain Creek?"

"Maybe so, Hooter. Who else is going? Mama will ask that right off the bat."

"Ol' Bubba an' Ridge an' Monkey-wrench. They've already said they'd go."

"Uh-oh. Trouble. I'll have to ask. Let me call you back."

"Okay. By the way, how's the 'nightly pinups' going?"

Travis hung up the phone to a round of rowdy laughter, more than a little irritated by his friend's jesting. Nevertheless, he really did want to go on the trip. Once they all got together, Hooter tended to pick on Bubba like everybody else did, and Travis's curls ceased to be an issue. On Sharp Mountain Creek there was a humongous cliff that had an ideal adjacent campsite. They could explore some caves in the cliff, put out bank hooks and trotlines in the creek, and if it were warm enough maybe they could do some grabbling for turtles underneath overhanging creek banks. Water temperature would still be cold, but predictions of warm days and the sure prospect of a blazing campfire beckoned.

As Travis expected, his mother was considerably less than enthusiastic about the expedition. She gave reluctant consent, realizing that her boy needed a break like this. Studies in his first year of high school had been more demanding than anything he had previously experienced, and he had struggled some with Spanish. She was afraid the absence of his father was having a telling effect, too. To boot, Travis had seemed somewhat melancholy in recent weeks, and she was a little worried about him. Maybe an adventure would do him some good. She extracted several stringent promises from him before consenting to his participation. Travis passed her positive decision on to Hooter and the trip was on.

Travis barely had time to gather up his sleeping quilt and cooking utensils before Hooter arrived in the old family Jeep with the others crowded aboard. The Jeep was piled high with supplies, leaving hardly any room for passengers. Somehow, they got all the necessary goods in and were shortly on their way.

"This is amazing! Your dad let you have the Jeep again! And you don't even have your driver's license yet," commented Travis as they motored down the rough road and bounced across the railroad tracks.

"It took a year and a half, but he finally gave in. I've got to stay on dirt roads all the way after we leave Indian Park. And Hoke knows all about it. Dad called him and got his okay. And ain't it just like you, Curly-top, to be bringing up little technicalities. Relax and have some fun for a change, huh?"

"Well, let's just park it so it stays on dry land. Sharp Mountain Creek runs a lot faster than the Etowah. Fast enough to wash this tin can clear to Alabama."

"You're right about that. We'll scotch the wheels and park 'er a half mile back. No, sir, we can't take a chance on another calamity with this Jeep," said Hooter with conviction.

"We kin drive right t' th' campsite," observed Bubba from his perch atop a mountain of supplies. "'An' 'en we kin drive it back out part-way an' tie it t' 'at big oak tree like a sway-back mule."

"Don't think that'll be necessary," said Hooter as they swung past the bank. "It ain't likely to go wanderin' off grazin'."

Banker Barksdale was out in front of the bank, preparing to lock up for the day. Poss Wilson was just pulling away from the bank in a brand-new Ford pickup truck, and Hooter whistled low as the shiny machine eased by them.

"Man, those Wilsons are either rolling in dough or they're up to their ears in debt. I saw Dead Bird and Razz in a new pickup a couple of days ago, too. They bought a new television and a new refrigerator from Dad just last week, and they paid cash for them. They come to the bank pretty often, so they must be getting paid good at the sawmill."

"Sawmill work don't pay nobody good. 'Ey's somethin' funny goin' on wi' 'at bunch," observed Monkey-wrench. "M' daddy used t' work at 'at sawmill, an' I kin tell ye it's starvation wages."

"Sawmill work never has paid much, I guess," noted Travis. "Mr. McCard says he used to walk nine miles to work at the sawmill, and he got paid fifty cents a day. And he had two ways to get there..."

"Okay, okay," said Hooter, stopping him in mid-sentence as he swerved to miss a stray hound dog that was sitting smack in the center of the street, its long ears drooped nearly to the ground. "I've heard old Hank tell that one a hundred times, too, just like you have. And so has everybody else in Cherokee County."

"Well, maybe that means it's true. Anyway, the point is it's not likely those guys are making enough salary to buy new trucks and things like that. If they pooled all their money, it still wouldn't be enough to buy even one vehicle."

"Then whur's th' money coming fum? I wonder if Banker Barksdale knows," said Bubba.

"If he does, he won't likely tell you. Nor me, either. I bet Hoke's noticed them, and he'll get to the bottom of it," said Travis.

"I wouldn't say 'at. He ne'er did find out who shot Hunkie Ferby. Hoke's sharp on some thangs, like keeping up wi' who's driving when 'ey shouldn't, but 'e's not much o' a detective. I bet we could figger 'is all out if we put our minds t' it."

"Later," said Hooter as he sped down a narrow dirt road that led north out of town. "Right now we've got a tent to put up, trot lines to run, and a cliff to climb. And then supper to fix and who knows what else."

An ancient wooden bridge across the roaring creek was just ahead, and just before reaching it they turned across a greening pasture toward a distant mountain that was small but extremely vertical. They followed a weathered, muddy two-track for more than a mile, splashing through a shallow branch that required four-wheel-drive, before finally stopping at the base of a rocky, vertical face. Next to the campsite was a short strand of sand, and just below it Sharp Mountain Creek curved acutely along the cliff base, making a ninety degree turn in less than a stone's throw. From that point the water churned out of sight through dark timber downstream. The place was well worn by previous campers and fishermen, and they selected a flat area with a circle of stones already laid out for a campfire.

Shortly, a big, green army surplus tent was up, cozy quilts were laid out, and fishing lines were being readied. They rolled out one of the trotlines first, a device that consisted of a long strand of heavy gauge twine, from which dangled two-foot sections of smaller string. Each shorter section had a sharp hook at the end, and six inches or so above that was a half-ounce lead sinker. Some hooks were slightly rusted, and Hooter broke out a file from the Jeep's toolbox to sharpen them.

"Go back to the branch and catch some spring lizards, Curly-top," he instructed. "Take the Jeep, and maybe you could go with him,

Bubba."

"Okay," said Travis. He had received considerable instruction in straight shift driving since the time H.K. McCard was shot, and he felt well able to do the job. The Jeep clutch was different from his grandfather's old car, but he soon had it figured out and they bounced away.

Spring lizards were plentiful if one knew where to look. They inhabited places where the flow of water was slowed to a trickle, and preferred rocky locations where there were quiet pools here and there. By rummaging among the moss and turning over stones and rotting logs, the pair very quickly had their container writhing with healthy bait. Shortly Travis and Bubba were back at the campsite, and soon thereafter at least forty hooks were in the water to tempt the catfish of Sharp Mountain Creek. Now it was time for a little exploring.

The boys climbed like mountain goats, jumping from rock to rock and seeing who could get highest by the most dangerous route. The Jeep and the tent looked like toys down below by the time they topped out. Their trip down was mostly uneventful, except for some minor scrapes and bruises. Monkey-wrench was the heaviest and least agile of the group, and at one point he stumbled and twisted one of his tree-trunk knees. Aside from this, all five arrived safely back at camp.

Enough catfish had already been snared on the trotlines and bush hooks to provide supper, but they had also lost a lot of bait.

"Got to have some more spring lizards, guys," said Hooter "I want us to take some fish home tomorrow just to prove we were here."

"Let's go, Ridge," said Monkey-wrench. "We'll git plenty o' lizards. An' we're gonna do some grabbling along th' branch befo' we come back."

Grabbling was a dangerous way of foraging, but one could

sometimes catch turtles or really big fish by thrusting both bare hands into the underwater overhang of a stream bank. An experienced grabbler could tell what he was feeling before he grabbed it, and developed an uncanny ability to tell a catfish from a cottonmouth moccasin, as well as which end of a turtle could be seized safely. But the learning curve was steep and hazardous.

After catching another supply of lizards, Ridge grabbled up a big snapping turtle that was more than a foot in diameter. He narrowly escaped being bitten by a moccasin, the cold water and sluggish early-spring condition of the serpent saving him from harm. They took the container of lizards, as well as the snapping turtle, back to camp. There were plenty of fish to eat, and nobody particularly relished cleaning a turtle, so they elected to play "crush the stick" with the creature and its vise-like jaws before releasing it unharmed back into the chill waters of the main creek.

"'Is ol' Jeep still ain't been baptized 'is trip, Hooter," commented Ridge as he patted the hood of the vehicle. "Ort I park 'er a little closer t' th' water?"

"Nope, it's in fine condition right where it is," replied Hooter. "In fact, scotch the wheels with a couple of those rocks. We can't take any chances. It's a long walk out of here, and if that thing gets drowned I'll be grounded—forever."

Ridge and Monkey-wrench drew fish cleaning duties, and they chuckled every now and then as they skinned catfish. Their mirth bordered on outright glee as they prepared a fish especially for Bubba. Three sharp hooks were threaded into the selected specimen, with the eye of the hook cleverly concealed next to the backbone. They marked the booby-trapped fish with a notch in the back fin, and presented the fine platter to Hooter and Travis for cooking.

There was no obvious effort to steer the trick catfish toward Bubba, but it wound up on his plate through some deft maneuvering by Monkey-wrench and Ridge. Fried catfish is eaten like corn-on-the-cob, by picking up the whole fish and gnawing the flesh off the central spine of bone. Poor Bubba got through three bites before hitting one of the hooks, which he jammed deeply and painfully into his upper gum. He jumped up and looked as if he were doing a war dance around the campfire, holding his mouth and crying out in pain. Travis and Hooter were shocked, but both of them suspected immediately that Bubba's merciless cousins were somehow behind the episode. Travis took a flashlight and inspected the injury, and with some difficulty he was able to extract the hook with a pair of pliers from the Jeep.

"I'd throw 'at 'un back, Bubba," said Monkey-wrench, while he laughed so hard he could hardly get the words out. "Ain't much fun t' catch a fish 'at bites back, huh, cuz?"

"Yeah," Ridge chimed in, "I reckin somebody fergot t' take th' hook out'n 'at 'un!"

Both of them continued to roll around on the ground and laugh, while Bubba got a murderous look on his face as his pain abated. He gave both of them a benign kick, then went to the creek to wash accumulated blood out of his mouth.

"You guys are bad," said Hooter "I'm just glad Bubba didn't bring a gun."

"Aw, 'e won't do nothin'. 'E likes fer us t' kid 'im," said Monkey-wrench as his chuckles subsided. "He'd thank we didn't like 'im if we ne'er did nothin' like 'at."

"You ought to try it sometime and see," said Travis "By the way, did you booby-trap any more of these fish."

"Heck naw. It was hard enough t' make sho' th' right person got 'at un," said Ridge. "Le's eat. Hey, Bubba, come on back! Th' rest o' 'em s cleaned a mite better'n 'at 'un."

Bubba did return shortly, but he sulked and refused to eat for a while. Soon the aroma of tasty food overwhelmed his reluctance, and he gingerly reassembled a plate of food to replace the one he had spilled. He was far more careful as he bit into each fish, however, and the rest of the meal was uneventful. Around the roaring fire everyone filled up on fried catfish with all the trimmings, and soon the hook episode seemed forgotten. Danger on the adjacent high terrain had been an awesome thrill, and they verbally relived their climb repeatedly. Nippy night air closed in around them, and soon all of them were edging a little closer to the warm blaze. It was good to be out, good to be with friends, and good to have a full stomach. And it was good not to have a very sore mouth, thought Travis, ever so glad he had not been the recipient of that particular joke.

"Say, Hooter, whutcha thank 'bout 'em funny smokes 'ey're sellin' at Cherokee City High?" asked Monkey-wrench.

"Don't know. Never tried one. I don't like smoking," said Hooter. "But I heard some kid say they make you float like a butterfly."

"What are you guys talking about?" asked Travis, who had become somewhat sleepy with his full stomach and the soothing warmth from the fire.

"Funny smokes. Some o' th' guys are smokin' homemade cigarettes 'stead o' factory-made ones. My grandpa still rolls 'is own, so ain't nothin' wrong wi' 'em bein' homemade, don't reckin," said Monkey-wrench.

"Well, if they're selling smokes at school, it's still against the rules homemade or not," said Travis. "If it can't be sold in the canteen, it can' be sold there legally."

"Right, an' 'ey ain't s'posed t' sell factory-made cigarettes 'ere neither," noted Ridge. "But I kin buy 'em anyhow, whene'er I want. An 'is kid fum o'er Talkin' Rock way sells th' funny ones fum 'is book satchel. I got a pack right 'ere, if y' wan' t' see 'em."

He extracted a pack of the homemade cigarettes from his knapsack and passed it around. Travis pulled one of the strange smokes from the flat pack and looked it over carefully. It was readily apparent that there was no tobacco smell to it, instead being more sweet and pungent, and not in the least offensive to one's nose.

"Wan' t' light it, Curly-top?" asked Monkey-wrench as he lit up his own with an ember from the fire and leaned back against a big log with a satisfied look on his face.

"No, thanks. I don't need smoking. Not even when it's minus tobacco," he answered. Hooter declined the offer, too, but Bubba shortly joined Ridge and Monkey-wrench in puffing away. The aroma was entirely foreign to Travis, and he puzzled over this new forbidden fruit. Shortly Bubba was leaning back with his head draped over the back of the log and his mouth wide open, snoring loudly, while the other two talked louder and louder, filling the night woods with ringing human voices.

"Girls! We need girls here," said Monkey-wrench thickly, then he followed the comment with a thunderous, hearty laugh. "'At's whut's missin'. We need Trixie Wills 'ere wi'out Red Roper. Get in 'at Jeep and go git 'er, Hooter."

"I like your idea, but there's about as much chance of that as a bear having kittens. I don't want to die tonight, thanks," answered Hooter. "And you can't go, either. You're beginning to sound like you're drunk. Does that thing you're sucking on make you dizzy in the head?"

"I'm already purty dizzy in th' head. 'Ese cigs jes' make me a li'l' mo' like 'at. An' if'n ye ain't goin' adder Trixie, I'm gonna use 'at Jeep."

155

"No!" said Hooter firmly. "Even if you weren't acting crazy, I still wouldn't let you drive to Trixie's house. You'd get beaten to a pulp if Red were there, and probably get shot if he weren't. So forget it. You can fantasize about it, that's all."

"T' heck wi' *you!*" said Monkey-wrench firmly. "Me an' Ridge an' Bubba's going t' Trixie's. An' ye can't stop us. Right, guys?"

"Sounds good t' me," said Ridge dreamily as smoke curled in circles around his head. "Bubba's asleep, though."

"Bubba, wake up! We're goin' t' Trixie's house!" shouted Monkey-wrench, shaking the snoring boy, who barely roused enough to smile before sinking back into a deep sleep.

"Okay, we'll go, jes' th' two o' us," said Monkey-wrench. "Can't trust Bubba wi' nothin', not e'en t' stay awake. Shoulda put 'at hook in 'is nose. Come on, Ridge."

"See you in the morning, if you make it back," said Travis as the two stood to go. Before anyone could react, the two had jumped into the Jeep, and the engine started in the darkness.

"Hey!" yelled Hooter, leaping to his feet and running toward the sound. "I told you that Jeep's not going!"

Travis dashed after him, while Bubba sprawled sleeping and oblivious. When Travis reached the Jeep, there was a mad scramble in process over control of the steering wheel. Monkey-wrench let out the clutch, while Hooter grappled to try and turn off the ignition key. Travis went to the other side and waged a futile battle against a much-stronger Ridge, though he did somehow keep him from helping Monkey-wrench very much. The vehicle crept forward, bucking like a mule in a cocklebur patch. Neither Hooter nor Monkey-wrench could win the battle, which was rapidly turning dangerous. The advantage surged back and forth between Hooter's attempts to kill the engine and a struggle for command of the steering wheel. Travis jumped back when he saw that the vehicle was gaining momentum, and just escaped being run over when he tripped on an unexpected root.

"Doggone you, Monkey-wrench, let go the wheel!" Hooter yelled, while his adversary shouted back various colors of profanity as the Jeep moved forward with no one in undisputed control, missing sleeping Bubba and the blazing fire by mere inches. Down the steep bank it went, directly toward the noisy, churning creek. It crossed the sandbar upright, but capsized when it struck a huge boulder at water's edge. The rear of the vehicle was thrust almost straight up in the air, while the engine went completely submerged. Water poured into the open passenger side, virtually washing the two occupants out the driver's side. Hooter, who was unhurt, pummeled both of them unmercifully with his fists as they flowed out, bursting Monkey-wrench's lip in a bloody spray with a right, they punching Ridge with a left and a right and bloodying his nose. The two bigger and stronger boys were remarkably easy for him to handle, though he also did significant damage to his flailing hands.

"Now look what you've done! We'll never get the Jeep again! Look what you've done!" yelled Hooter again and again. "A trial run, said Dad. And you've ruined it!" He slugged both of them again in turn, wincing from pain in his knuckles.

Travis ran up with his flashlight, breathless, and surveyed the situation. To his relief, the Jeep was not going to wash away, apparently being firmly wedged against the boulder, and all three of his friends were alive with nothing missing or badly broken. He tried to separate Hooter from his final angry assault on the other two bleeding boys, but was accidentally smacked in the face, sending him reeling.

"Stop it, Hooter. Stop it! Everybody's all right!"

"You might be, but I'm ruined. Wait 'til Dad sees this. Again! This is the last time with this crew!"

Monkey-wrench and Ridge sat mute on the sand as Hooter's anger slowly but reluctantly subsided, while Travis surveyed the situation more thoroughly with his light. On seeing clearly that the engine was well submerged, Hooter's hot anger flared again, and he seemed about to light into the pair again. The cold water had sobered the brothers considerably, but they still seemed to be fuzzy in their thinking. As the reality of the wreck sank in, they lapsed virtually into complete silence.

"Thanks again, guys," said Hooter icily as he climbed the bank toward the campfire where Bubba was still sleeping, totally ignorant of his brush with death. "I'm going to walk to town and get help. The longer that engine stays under water, the worse the repairs. I found that out before, unfortunately."

"I'll go with you, Hooter," said Travis "I'll never be able to sleep around here anyway."

"I think you'd better stay here," he said with amazing clarity of thought. "These guys need a doctor in the house for right now. Let's not leave them alone."

"Durn you, Hooter, I los' m' smokes," Ridge called after them in slurred, hazy tones. "Cost me ten dollars, 'at pack o' smokes. An' 'ey's gone. Gone."

"Good riddance!" yelled Hooter. "And good luck to you, Curly-top. Take care of 'em, I might want to beat on 'em some more when I get back. It'll take me better'n two hours to reach town, and who knows how long to find Graham's tow truck driver. But we've got to get that Jeep out. Man, I hate to tell Dad about this!"

"I can vouch that it wasn't your fault. Maybe that'll help."

"Maybe. But it wasn't my fault last time, either. The parking brake failed," said Hooter, rubbing his swelling knuckles. "Darn these yo-yos and their funny smokes, whatever they are. But I still don't think Dad will be very impressed with any excuses."

Shortly Travis could see his friend's lonely flashlight disappearing into distant blackness as he directed two wet, cold boys into the tent and the warmth of dry clothes and comforting quilts. With some effort he was able to rouse Bubba and get him inside, too. Within minutes, there was loud snoring reverberating within the tent, the sheer force of it almost causing the canvas to pulsate. It was going to be a long night for one skinny outdoorsman.

He couldn't sleep, so perhaps it was out of boredom that he prayed. He prayed for his friend who was walking to find help. And he prayed for the three boys asleep around him. And for some reason, as he lay awake surrounded by black darkness, he was moved to pray a special prayer for his old friend, Hank McCard.

CHAPTER 14

Consequences related to that night at Sharp Mountain Creek were far-reaching, and quite justly resulted in less pain and suffering for Hooter and Travis than it did for the other three boys. When the Jeep was finally retrieved around 3:00 A.M., Monkey-wrench, Ridge, and Bubba had pretty well slept off the effects of their smoking habits. They pitched in and helped Jabo Kellett, who drove a big towing rig for Graham Motor Company, as he gingerly plucked the Jeep from the frigid water. Relatively little damage had been done, and after draining the distributor cap and letting the whole outfit dry out under a fan in Graham's garage, it actually cranked the next day. There were few mechanical parts in need of repair, though the interior and everything under the hood had been soaked.

Since it had been a vehicle accident, Kellett had been required to call the local lawman, Hoke Hatfield, who duly investigated. Hooter made every effort to downplay his friends' roles, but it eventually came out that there had been a level of drunkenness in their actions, despite absence of any alcohol in the camp. His inquiry and ultimate unraveling of the story led inevitably to Cherokee City High principal Evan Theobold, whose school was reportedly the source of those "funny smokes" that had led to near-disaster.

Theobold was known to students as the "Bald Eagle of Cherokee," since he had not a single hair on his head. He had huge, drooping jowls like a bulldog, and his frowning, intense face and a pair of rigid unblinking eyes made his nickname all the more apt. His stout frame and firm, noncompromising demeanor struck fear into the heart of any student caught in transgression, as he was a disciplinarian of the first order. On Monday after the incident, he had all five boys in his office for interrogation, and their parents were required to be there as well. The whole affair caused quite a stir around school, and made holding meaningful classes that day quite difficult. A man none of the boys knew sat in on the fact-finding session, staying in one corner and saying nothing as Theobold asked a series of pertinent questions. Before the day was out, the boy from Talking Rock had been arrested for distribution of an illegal substance. Monky-wrench, Ridge, and Bubba were charged with misdemeanor possession of marijuana, and soon a court date was in the offing for all of them. The seller was expelled from school and carted away in a police car, while the three smokers were given corporeal punishment, followed by appropriate suspensions.

Travis and Hooter were completely exonerated of wrongdoing, but the episode nevertheless had a telling effect on both of them. Innocence had been stripped away as they learned the devastating consequences of violating the law. They came away with a determination to avoid such calamities in the future. Each one further resolved that they had taken their last camping excursion with the McTaggart brothers and their cousin. Hooter suffered a broken knuckle from slugging his erstwhile friends, and for many days his right hand was so swollen he had difficulty writing, eating, and working in the store.

"Honest to goodness, Mama, I never heard of marijuana," said Travis as they drove home from the inquisition. "Well, maybe in Spanish class when we sing La Cucaracha, but I really didn't know what it was or what it did to people."

"I do, and I did before this happened. Your father spent a lot of time in Panama before and during the war, and he's told me about how it grows wild down there, and how the natives use it as a smoke. I've heard him say it would make you as drunk as a coon on a log. I never thought about it ever showing up here in Cherokee County, though."

"Well, I sure didn't know what it was. I wonder where that kid got that stuff."

"We'll just have to leave that up to Hoke and the county sheriff's department. And the Georgia Bureau of Investigation. That fellow who was there while Mr. Theobold was talking with you boys is a GBI agent."

"Oh, wow. He sure didn't say much. I thought he was from the county sheriff's department. I wonder what else they're going to do to that boy who sold the stuff."

"I think they'll try to get him to lead them to his supplier. If they don't find out who's providing the stuff, all that will happen is that some other kid will wind up selling it."

Sobering thoughts coursed through Travis's mind as they drove home, and he was extremely thankful that he had not been hurt in the flurry of madness that had descended on their camping trip. Was it his guardian angel? It had been such a melee, and he didn't remember any sense of a protective presence this time. Surely there had been someone looking after him when he had tripped and fallen beside the moving Jeep. He sat mostly in silence as they drove home, and before long they were headed up the steep dirt hill past the Wilson place. None of the men or vehicles was evident today.

"Mama, can I go visit Mr. McCard?"

"Get your homework, then after supper you can go if you want."

Travis later walked into the old man's yard, and from afar he could see Hank sitting in his usual position, rocking with his legs crossed in typical pose. The evening was as clear as crystal glass, and a grand yellow sun was setting behind the big burned area across the road.

"Hi, Mr. McCard!"

"Evenin', son. Come up an' set a spell."

"Don't mind if I do. Everything okay?"

"Nope. Ain't got no dogs no mo'. Foun' bouf o' 'em dead 'is mornin'. Kilt fer spite. An' I know 'zackly who did it."

"What? Bruno and Spot? Dead?"

"Yep. Dead as a chicken's second day away fum home. P'ison o' some kind, prob'ly struck wi' strick-nine."

"Who would do something like that? And why?"

"Runt Mayberry, er maybe 'is boy. 'Ey wuz up couple o' days ago wantin' to raid Gracie an' Teddy's chicken houses fer th' ten hunnerth time, an' I tol' 'em no mo'. 'Ey jes' plain been used t' takin' whut 'ey wanted when 'ey wanted 'em. An' I tol' ol' Runt if'n 'e wanted t' turn me in fer shootin' 'at revenooer, t' jes' go ahead an' call Hoke. 'Cause I'm through curtseyin' t' 'at bunch, now 'at Maggie's gone. I druther perish in th' pokey, fer all th' good it'll do 'em t' lock me up. An' I be dog if'n 'ey wuzn't madder'n a wil'cat in a steel trap when I tol' 'em 'at."

"And you think they killed Spot and Bruno because you wouldn't let them have any more free chickens?"

"Ain't no question 'bout it, son. I'm a ol' man, an' it wouldn't be much pleasure t' Runt t' see me locked away nohow. Ain't got 'at many days lef', ye see. So 'e up 'n' kilt th' bes' two dogs 'is side o' Atlanta. 'At riff-raff bunch o' feists 'e's got ain't worth shootin'. An' 'e always wuz jealous o' m' dogs."

"That's awful," said Travis, shaking his head, his voice quivering ever so slightly.

"Tain't like 'em dogs wuz th' bes' 'ey e'er wuz, nohow, but I sho' am gonna miss 'em. Don't reckin I'll ne'er have nary 'nother dog o' no kind. I'd sho' like t' find one o' 'em ol'-fashioned cur dogs, if'n I e'er got 'nother dog. Don't reckin at's e'er gon' happen, though. 'At kind is hard t' find 'ese days. I've heered tell 'ey's some o' 'em up in Dawson County, back in th' backwoods."

"I wouldn't know about that. Wow. Bruno and Spot dead," said Travis again as a tear trickled down his cheek. "I can't believe it, Mr. McCard. What did you do with them?"

"Teddy he'ped me bury 'em, o'er by 'em hickernut trees, jes' befo' y' get t' th' chinkypin ridge. 'E wuz able t' drive 'is truck might nigh t' th' spot. 'Em dogs treed a many a squirrel in 'at section."

"They sure did. Oh, Mr. McCard, what are we going to do? Can't we tell Hoke?" asked Travis, wiping his eyes with the back of his hand.

"'Twon't do no good. I ain't got no proof. But we'll make it, boy. If'n worse comes t' worse, we kin sit down and still hunt. 'Taint nigh as much fun, but it puts squirrels in th' pot. An' m' ol' legs ain't up t' walkin' s' much nowadays nohow. I do hope ol' Runt gets 'is due somehow. Drivin' up 'ere in a brand-new pickup truck an' demandin' a pile o' fresh chicken like 'e owns th' place. Wal, I done had enough o' 'is demandin'. Druther eat a piece o' mad dog 'an a piece o' chicken, m'se'f. But Teddy works like a slave in 'at hot ol' broiler house, an' I be dog if'n I wouldn' druther spend th' rest o' m' days in jail as t' give Runt Mayberry 'nother feather off'n one o' 'em chickens."

Travis had intended to tell his friend about the disastrous camping trip to Sharp Mountain Creek, but he thought better of it and decided to keep it to himself. For the moment it seemed better to simply not discuss any other negative news. It wasn't long before he walked slowly toward home, carrying a burden that seemed like a knapsack full of bricks. Should he tell his mother any of what he knew about Hank's past? No, he couldn't betray the trust Hank had bestowed on him. He could tell her some things, though, but not the most important ones. This particular day she had already been put through a full-scale investigation of marijuana sales at Cherokee City High. It would be too much to tell her more about Mr. McCard's past.

"Mama, somebody poisoned Bruno and Spot," he said as he walked into the house. "Mr. McCard and Teddy buried both of them out back of the burn. Mr. McCard's pretty sad about it. And so am I."

"Oh, my goodness, I'm sorry. Actually, son, I have to tell you, I already knew about it. Gracie called me this morning at work and told me, before I left to go to Cherokee City. I just decided to let Mr. McCard tell you. Son, there are some petty, mean people in this world. You need to stay away from that kind."

"You're right about that, Mama. He thinks the Mayberrys did it."

"Really? Why does he think that?"

"Well, it's pretty complicated. And it goes back a long ways. And I just can't say much more about it, Mama. Mr. McCard told me the whole story in confidence, just between us men."

"Oh, I see. Well, I certainly understand. And I hope somehow they get what's coming to them. Whoever did it was heartless and cruel, to say the least."

"I agree, Mama," said Travis, shaking his head and turning his eyes downward as another tear clouded his vision. He went to the window and looked down the hill toward the spring, where dogwoods were now blooming and luxurious pale green dominated the scene. A thought occurred to him as he gazed at the verdant world outside.

"Mama, can we get Mr. McCard another dog? One time he had an old-fashioned cur dog that he loved. Best dog he ever had. If he had one, I think he'd feel a little better. S'pose we could find him a cur dog?"

"I wouldn't know where to look, Travis, would you? I don't even know if that's a real breed or not."

"Oh, it's a real breed, all right. You have to get them 'way up in the mountains, where there's not much opportunity for mixing with inferior breeds. Mr. McCard says there's still some of them to be had, if a fellow looks hard enough."

"Sounds like a project we could attempt. A little driving around up in Gilmer and Fannin Counties might be fun, and we really ought to go visit the old home place up in Dawson County. We've got lots of relatives in those parts."

"Please call some of them, Mama. Mr. McCard said tonight he'd heard there were some in the backwoods of Dawson County, but he also said they're hard to find. Having a real cur dog is the only thing that might really make him feel happy again. Get some of our folks to ask around."

"Maybe we'll do that, son. But we can't do it this weekend. I have to take Bobby and Sue to get new shoes, and I need you to pick a mess of poke salad. The big burn is growing up so so deep in new growth that I don't guess there'll be much out there this year. Got any ideas on where to get a basket full?"

"If you'll be thinking on that cur dog, I'll be thinking on the poke salad. That old sawdust pile near chinkypin ridge might be a real possibility. Matter of fact, Mr. McCard mentioned while we were squirrel hunting last winter that it would be a good place to find it, come spring."

"Maybe Saturday you can take a walk over there and see if it's up yet. It usually gets going good by this time of year."

"Maybe Mr. McCard would like to go with me," mulled Travis before heading off to prepare for bed. "I'll walk up there later this week and talk to him about getting him a cur dog, and I'll see if he wants to go with me to the sawdust pile this weekend."

Travis had every intention of doing exactly that, but for some reason he was never able to get around to it. There was an extra Boy Scout meeting that week, and his Spanish class was driving him crazy with homework. Before he knew it, it was after dark on Friday evening, and already too late to walk down the road to visit his friend. And Mr. McCard never talked on the phone, so it was useless to try and call him. Besides, he knew his friend would already be in bed.

He'd get up early on Saturday morning and go by on his way to pick poke salad, and see if Hank wanted to go with him.

CHAPTER 15

"Mr. McCard!" called Travis as he knocked on the front door of the white wooden house where his old friend lived. There was no response, so after waiting, shouting, and knocking again he went to the back door. Again, there was no answer. Gracie, who lived next door, finally heard Travis and came over to see what was causing the commotion. Alarmed that her father had not answered the knocking and shouting, she went into the house, hoping he was not ill, or worse. There was nobody home.

"He must have walked off somewhere. Maybe to check on how the blackberries are blooming. You know he'll have the best places scouted out long before the weather gets hot."

"Yeah, I reckon you're right, Gracie. Thanks for coming over. I just wanted to see if he'd like to go with me to gather poke salad over by the sawdust pile the other side of the burn."

"I'm sure he would. He isn't walking as well as he used to, but he still likes to get out and about. If you're going that direction, I'd bet you might run into him. If he comes back before you do, I'll tell him you were here. But don't worry about him. If he weren't well, he'd be right here."

Travis bid her good day and started down a well-worn trail that led across the burn. A high wall of second-growth brush had formed on both sides of an old logging road, and here and there blackened snags aimed skyward. He stepped over rotting timbers at intervals, dodged aggressive brush on both sides of the path, and kept a wary eye out for snakes. After some vigorous walking he broke into a small opening where the sawdust pile was located. Indeed, as expected, tender young poke weed grew thick all around the site, and filling his basket would be a simple matter of a few minutes.

Far away toward the river, he could hear something unusual, and he stood quietly for a second, wondering what it might be. Was that the faint sound of a motor running? He cocked his head and listened, cupping one hand over his ear. There could be no doubt about it. It was unquestionably the deep-throated roar of a diesel engine, and by his reckoning it was coming from somewhere in the vicinity of that dangerous clearing where he had seen the tractor and Jeep. He listened for a couple of minutes while he tentatively picked several stalks of poke salad and deposited them in his basket. The roar continued unabated, and after a while he could stand it no more. He put down his basket and climbed up on top of a big, flat-topped charcoal stump to gain a little higher perspective. Listening again, he was now certain. It had to be that tractor he had seen last winter.

Dare he investigate? He involuntarily reached and felt of his arm, where a little knot of scarring persisted from his superficial gunshot wound. He considered the irate shooters he had incited last winter, and he decided it would be dangerous to intrude on their territory again. He climbed down and finished filling up his basket, trying to ignore the sound, but his persistent inquisitive thoughts wouldn't go away. Finally, he walked tentatively toward the engine noise, and it became even more distinct. He set his basket in a shady place underneath a large hickory tree and contemplated. He ultimately decided that he would go just a little ways closer, enough perhaps to see exactly what was going on, but not close enough for anyone to know he was there.

He eased along the chinquapin ridge like a stalking cat, and then dropped down next to a flowing branch that paralleled higher ground. Noisy, rushing water greatly muffled the distant engine sound, but it also concealed his footfall in dry leaves underfoot. It was scary when the waters flattened out in broad bottomland nearer the river, and the masking sound likewise abated. In contrast, the tractor motor sounded ever closer, but he still couldn't see the field, much less the tractor and its driver. With the advent of new foliage, and bursting of countless leafy buds on spring brush, the landscape had radically changed since his narrow escape here. He felt some trepidation as it became apparent that he would have to get much closer than his comfort level allowed in order to find out who was on that tractor and what they were doing. He was ever more fearful, but he was driven relentlessly by intense curiosity. His heart raced as he eased along, sneaking like an Indian scout in a Western movie, but he never seriously considering turning back.

Finally, he could see the opening up ahead. He got down on his hands and knees and crawled the last several yards, and his eyes widened dramatically at the sight. A dump truck mounded up with chicken litter was unloading, while the tractor driver spread piles of the stuff across the field with a blade and tilled it into the soil. Between them and his location Travis could see row after row of growing green plants, already standing a foot tall and reaching skyward like the pokeweed he had been gathering a short time before. The leaves on the plants were fragile in appearance, long and skinny and shaped somewhat like poison ivy. One of the rows ended just in front of him, and he chanced reaching out and pulling one of the thin leaves.

He rolled the shiny leaf between his fingers, inspecting it carefully. He crushed the leaf until it capitulated into a small, green ball, then he put it to his nose. The scent was vaguely familiar, and brought back memories of—what? It quickly dawned on him—marijuana! He should have guessed! Why hadn't he thought of that before?

His mind raced as he tried to settle on what to do next, and he hesitated briefly. He decided he had to run back, find Hoke, and show him physical evidence of this illicit farm. He leaned forward and pulled a whole leaf, and with it clutched in his hand he started crawling backwards.

He ran into something as he backed up, something hard and unyielding. The object shoved back vigorously, almost knocking the breath out of him and sending him rolling. Terrified, he whirled to see what was happening. What suddenly dominated his vision evoked a horror that bordered on hysteria, and he let out an involuntary cry that welled from deep within. Runt Mayberry was standing over him, a twisted scowl on his face, holding his .22 automatic rifle in ready position. He had the barrel pointed directly at Travis's face, only inches away.

"What ye doin' 'ere, boy?" demanded Runt, shaking the rifle barrel wickedly in front of his eyes and delivering a slap to his face that tumbled Travis backward again. "I see ye done stole some o' m' crop, too. Don't ye know 'at's a recipe fer trouble, kid? An' ye's up t' yo' ears in it."

"I'm sorry, Mr. Mayberry. I didn't mean any harm. Honest!" the boy cried, fear welling up into sudden, spontaneous tears.

"Wal', 'at's jes' too bad, now, ain't it? If'n ye thank ye kin jes' bawl an' tawk yo' way out'n 'is, ye got 'nother thank comin', Mister Smarty-pants. Now, git up slow an' easy an' wawk t'ward 'at field ye wuz stealin' out'n."

Travis complied, while at the same time he tried to clear his mind and control his emotions. He mentally kicked himself over and over for coming here in the first place, and to boot being stupid enough to get caught. A deep dread seized him as he remembered the bullet-riddled body of Hunkie Ferby, which they had stumbled on just a couple of miles upriver from this spot. His head spun as he dwelt on that hideous thought, and for a confused minute he was afraid he might actually pass out. He fought to remain conscious, realizing that if he swooned he might have no chance at all. His close call with the rattlesnake last year, and the words of Mr. McCard about his brush with disaster, echoed back in his mind. Staying alert and keeping cool seemed futile, but otherwise all would certainly be lost.

He broke into the open, Runt following close behind, and they were immediately spotted by the other men working the field. Dead Bird Wilson shut down the tractor engine, and Mutt Mayberry climbed down out of the dump truck. Poss Wilson and his other son, Razz, arrived from somewhere behind the sheds. They surrounded a shivering, terrified Travis, all of them glowering at this unwelcome intrusion.

"I tol' ye 'at wuz who we wuz shootin' at las' winter, Pappy," said Mutt. "'E hunts th' woods 'roun' 'ere all th' time. I knowed it wuz 'im."

"I ne'er said it warn't 'im, did I? Did ye e'er heah me say it warn't 'im?"

"No, Pappy, but ye didn' say it wuz, neither. We got t' kill 'im, ain't we?"

"Who's runnin' 'is operation, me er you? I'm gon' decide who gits kilt, an' who don't," said Runt, glowering at his son. "Might be we kin let 'im go, if'n we kin trust 'im t' say nothin'."

"I won't say nothin', nothin' at all, Mr. Mayberry," said Travis "You can grow whatever you want, marijuana or anything else out here, and I won't tell anybody, I promise."

"How'd ye know whut 'is stuff is, anyhow, boy?" roared Runt, anger flaring like brush ablaze. Travis shrank back in terror once more as the man shouted in his face. "Ye're sich a smarty-pants, fer sich a skinny bit o' nothin'! Set down right 'ere and right now on 'at pile o' manure! Razz, hol' 'is gun on 'im whilst we reckin a li'l'. Private-like, I mean."

Travis couldn't tell what was going on as the other four moved away from where he sat on a dark mound next to freshly plowed earth The intense, urine-like smell of chicken droppings burned in his nostrils making his eyes water and his nose run. Razz glowered at him with a hate that seemed palpable, and Travis wondered whether the angry youth might be the one who would shoot him, if that were the decision of the impromptu tribunal. Travis was certain that Razz would surely enjoy the deed, if the raging fire in his eyes were an accurate reflection of what was in his heart.

Shortly, the other four men sauntered back, and there was detectable swagger in Runt Mayberry's step. He first frowned at Travis his small eyes narrowed with malice, and then he spoke.

"Ye an' Razz gonna take a wawk wi' Dead Bird," said Runt, motioning the boy to his feet. "Don't ne'er wan' t' catch ye 'ere 'gin, an' we won't."

The meaning in his voice was unmistakable. Dread seized Travis, and he was on the verge of crying once more as he looked up into his captor's unyielding eyes. He prayed down deep in his heart for mercy, some of it spoken without words and some of it out loud, probably babbling so indistinctly that it meant little to the marijuana farmers. He struggled to right himself per orders, while Runt took the rifle from Razz and checked it carefully. The weapon used only .22 shorts, so it wasn't very potent, but it held a couple of dozen rounds that could be squeezed off as fast as one could pull the trigger. Satisifed the rifle was fully loaded, he looked down the barrel at the boy, and was about to hand it back to Razz. As this was transpiring, Travis underwent a quiet, inexplicable internal transformation. He felt a sudden, perceptible calm descend upon him, a security that he had experienced before in times of trouble. It was that undefinable Presence again! The boy's speech became unexpectedly emboldened, and his confidence soared. Even considering that he had nothing to lose, he still couldn't believe the words he heard coming from his own mouth.

"You people are up to no good, and you're going to pay for it. If I hadn't caught you, somebody else would have. How long do you think you're going to get away with this? And after you kill me, can you imagine how many agents will descend on this place? They'll bring airplanes and dogs and policemen and they won't stop until you're all found. You killed Hunkie, too, didn't you? Don't you think they already suspect that? They're already watching you, you know."

"'Ey ain't ne'er gonna find yo' skinny carcass, kid," said Razz icily. "An' Runt shot Hunkie 'cause he wuz a-fixin' t' wawk out on us. Tol' us we'd hafta answer t' Hoke! We ain't answerin' t' nobody, Smarty pants. Ye kin be sho' o' 'at."

"They'll find you, all right," said Travis firmly and with absolute conviction. His mind flashed to the wicker basket full of pokeweed he'd left, positioned such that it actually indicated which direction he'd gone from the sawdust pile. "I've even left some clues for the sheriff and the GBI. You're already caught. You may get some pleasure out of killing me, but you'll pay. I promise."

A cold shiver coursed the boy's spine as he said the words. The Presence was there, and it was palpable. He couldn't explain it, but his fear had vanished and he didn't feel afraid. Runt shoved the rifle barrel to within an inch of his face, and growled through the most menacing face imaginable.

"Now ye done it, boy! Ye's made me mad! I'm a mind t' do th' job m'sef, like I done ol' Hunkie, ye keep tawkin'!"

"Ye boys put 'at rifle down, an' be quick 'bout it," came a chill, assertive voice from thick bushes along the field edge. "Do it, er I'm liable t' start shootin' m'se'f."

"Who in tarnation is ye?" asked Runt. "Ye sho' sound a lot like 'at ol' buzzard, Hank McCard. Come on out an' act like a man, ye varmi't."

"'An' let ye kill me an' th' boy, too, Runt? Ain't no way. I got ye dead t' rights. Drop 'at peashooter! Now!"

Runt let the rifle go limp, pretending to release the weapon. As it was about to slide from his grasp, though, he readjusted his grip and instead grabbed Travis. He wrestled the boy in front of him, between himself and the sound of the voice, and put the barrel tight against the boy's throat.

"Now le's see ye step out, ye chicken snake," he threatened, pushing the gun barrel roughly into Travis's gullet. "If'n ye don't, 'is kid's dead…"

There was a sudden sharp crack, the familiar explosive bang of a .22 cartridge. Almost simultaneously with the pop of the rifle, a small round red spot appeared exactly centered between Runt Mayberry's dark eyebrows, and a tiny piece of lead scrambled his brain. Dead on his feet, he slumped to the ground, and his rifle slipped harmlessly out of his grasp. Travis felt his grip relax instantly, and he sprang away from Runt and the menacing weapon. The metallic clank of a pump rifle being reloaded echoed immediately from the brush. The boy's other captors wore stunned, terrified expressions, and none of them had time to move.

"One step t'wards 'at boy an' 'ey's 'nothern dead," came the ice-cold voice. "Boy, pick up 'at rifle an' wawk slow and easy o'er t'ward th' sheds. An' stay out'n th' line o' fire so's I kin put 'nothern down if'n 'eys dumb as a fence post, er if'n 'ey don't hear s' good."

"I'm moving, I'm moving," called Travis, stooping and pulling the weapon free from its entanglement in the dead man's arms. Runt Mayberry lay completely motionless, his head resting in a gathering puddle of crimson. The other four men stretched their arms instinctively skyward to show their determination not to challenge the hidden marksman.

As soon as Travis had cleared out of the way, a stooped figure arose from the thicket, his felt hat slightly askew on his head, and a prominent drop of sweat hanging precariously from his hooked nose. He walked slowly toward the men, keeping his old .22 pump at ready lest any should make an aggressive move.

"Come on back, now, boy. Jes' stay b'hin' me, jes' in case I hafta take out 'nothern," said Hank, never taking his eyes off his captives. "All ye vermin git face down in th' chicken leavin's, an' don't let me see ye move nary a feather. Boy, how fast ye reckin ye kin git t' town an' fetch ol' Hoke?"

"Mighty fast, Mr. McCard. Wow, what a great shot! You saved my life!"

"Is 'at a fack? Good thang I brung along m' ol' squirrel gun, jes' in case I runned into some kind o' snake. An' I sho' 'nuff did 'at, aw-rite. Now git, an' le's see if'n ye can't brang ol' Hoke right 'ere in less'n a hour."

"Keep your gun on 'em, Mr. McCard, and I'll run like the wind. If there's one thing I can do, it's run!"

"'Ey's lots o' thangs ye kin do, boy. An' lots ye already done. But try 'at runnin' right now, and don't stop t' smell th' flowers. 'Is ol' man ain't good fer too much time in th' sun."

Travis glanced back once over his shoulder at the men sprawled face down, and then he sprinted across the field and into thick vegetation. He ascended the chinquapin ridge in record time and dashed headlong across the burn, not even stopping to retrieve his basket of poke salad. Before long he was running up to the McCard house, which was a quarter-mile closer than his own home. While panting for breath he explained to a bewildered Gracie why they needed the sheriff, and badly. While she called, Travis ran on down the road, and by the time he arrived at his house Hoke was already coming up the dirt road, trailing a plume of agitated dust.

In order to get the lawman's car to the scene, they had to approach the marijuana fields by way of the old river road that went by the abandoned house. Hank was still in charge when they arrived, feeble but alert, guarding his prisoners like a cat on a mouse. Hoke barely had enough handcuffs to go around, but he had already radioed for help, and shortly the whole field was swarming with Cherokee County deputies. A big, black hearse, used in most mountain communities as an ambulance, made a long, treacherous drive down the narrow road to retrieve Runt Mayberry's body. A deputy gave Hank and Travis a ride home after all the commotion had died down. As they rode, Hank seemed to have recovered some from the exertion and mental stress of the day, and he seemed unusually talkative.

"Y' sho' 'nuff run 'at couple o' miles faster'n a scalded dog, boy," he complimented. "R'minds me o' back when I had t' wawk nine miles t' work at th' sawmill. I used t' work fer fifty cents a day 'ere. An' I had two ways o' gettin' 'ere, I could wawk—OR—I could run. An' if'n I wuz a minute late, it'd show up on m' paycheck. Ain't ye glad ye don'thafta do 'at?"

"I am, Mr. McCard. But I'm glad I could do a couple of fast miles. And thanks for saving my life."

"Thank nothin' o' it, son. Ol' Runt had it comin', if'n anybody did. I knowed he wuz gonna kill ye when I seed 'im turn ye o'er t' Razz. Razz is th' one whut shot ol' Hunkie Ferby, I'd wager. 'E's a mean 'un."

"Nope, Runt owned up to it while they had me under the gun. That's prob'ly the only good thing that happened today, as far as Razz is concerned."

"Is 'at so? Don't s'prise me none. But it wouldn't o' s'prised me none th' other way, neither."

That night Travis, always a light sleeper, had great difficulty drifting off. When he finally did go to sleep, he dreamed vivid dreams of heavily fertilized marijuana fields, wicked villains, narrow escapes, and rescue by dear friends. And always there was that Presence, somewhere in the background, keeping watch over him.

And it seemed to him that the Presence supervised him while he finally got a very good night's sleep.

CHAPTER 16

"Well, boy, come on in an' set a spell," said Hank as Travis finished his late afternoon trek up the dirt road and crossed his friend's yard.

A couple of weeks had passed since that fateful encounter with the marijuana growers, and the boy had seen the old man only briefly in the interval. It had rained almost every day since, keeping the dirt road muddy and inhospitable, so visits had been limited. With all the recent moisture, grass was growing vigorously, and the boy kicked at the shoetop high lawn as he crossed the yard and climbed a short flight of rickety steps.

"Don't mind if I do, Mr. McCard," said Travis. "I need a rest. That Spanish at school is driving me nuts. And the teacher just keeps on pushing me and won't let up. Maybe I'll survive, but I'll sure be glad when school's out. Oh, I just want to tell you again how much I appreciate what you did for me the other week."

"Ye knows ye's welcome, son. I done said ol' Runt had it comin', an' 'e did. It wuz a job 'at had t' be done. An' I happened t' be th' feller 'at had t' do it."

"By the way, I've been meaning to ask you, why were you all the way over there on the back of the Hoechst place that day, anyway? That's a mighty long ways to walk."

"Ye mean it's a mighty fur piece fer a ol' goat like me. Ye's th cause o' 'at, too, boy. I figgered 'ey wuz doin' somethin' outside th' law when ye tol' me 'bout somebody a-shootin' at ye. 'Ey ain't 'at many people in 'ese parts whut starts a-throwin' lead fer no reason a-tall, so suspicioned 'at bunch all along. Adder Runt kilt m' dogs, er else had 'em kilt, I jes' had t' see fer m'se'f whut 'at chicken manure fertilizin operation wuz all 'bout. Good thang I did."

"I'll say. You feeling okay, Mr. McCard?"

"Me? Sho' am, son. Like I jes' had a bate o' cracklin' bread an' taters. Which I ain't, but I feels purty good anyhow."

"You look a little pale to me. And you're sweating. You been out walking?"

"Nope. Been settin' right 'ere might nigh all day. It's jes' a li'l' hot, 'at's all."

"Anyway, thanks for being there when I needed you. I've got a feeling I'd be a missing person right now if it hadn't been for you."

"An' ne'er found, mos' likely. 'Ey's ol' water wells all over 'at country, an' a scoop o' dirt by 'at tractor in on top o' a feller fixes it 'til doomsday. It's a wonder 'ey didn' put ol' Hunkie in one o' 'em. I tol' ye 'at bunch warn't all 'at smart, e'en if'n 'ey did make a lot o' money selling 'at funny smokin' stuff."

"I understand there's all kinds of strategizing going on among the lawyers. Dead Bird's blaming Runt, and he's also fingered him as being the ringleader, which he was. And he's blaming Razz for doing most of the marketing and handling all the money. And all of them are blaming Mutt for bringing home those marijuana seeds from Panama. Razz is claiming he didn't know they were doing anything illegal, that he was just along because he was a hired hand. At least they're keeping all of them locked up."

"Hmph. A hired hand wi' a new pickup, 'e wuz. Brothers will be brothers, I reckin, son. Bein' loyal is jes' skin deep in some people. 'Eys all gon' spend time in th' big house, I'd wager."

"I'm glad Mr. Hoechst wasn't involved. He was absolutely livid when he learned they were moving chicken dirt from his depository and putting it on another part of his land. The Hoechsts are a hard-working family, and very honest, I think, so I'm glad they weren't a part of the operation."

"'Ey got all th' kids at Cherokee City High, I unnerstan', whut wuz sellin' th' weed, too. Good riddance, I'd say," said Hank. "An' son, I got one mo' thang I wan' t' tell ye 'bout. I had a tawk wi' ol' Hoke yestiddy, an' I give 'im all th' facks I knowed, an' 'en I tol' 'im 'bout killin' 'at revenooer way back, too, I did."

"You did? Is he going to charge you?"

"Nope. Said 'ey warn't no witnesses, an' th' case is closed as fur as he's concerned. 'E said if'n 'e wuz me, 'e'd keep it t' m'se'f an' say no mo' 'bout it. An' on th' advice o' a upstandin' lawman, 'at's whut I intends t' do."

"Well, you can count on me, Mr. McCard. I guess Hoke and me are the only people alive who know the whole story. Except God himself."

"Ay-uh, he knows, fer sho'," said Hank, averting his gaze back to the broad expanse of the now-verdant burned area. "I finally feels a whole sight better 'bout th' whole thang. An' maybe I'll excape th' wrath o' man. But ye can't excape th' wrath o' th' Almighty."

"Oh, yes, you can, Mr. McCard. Jesus is the way. No matter what a person's done. That's what that preacher from Atlanta said. And you know, I didn't even know for sure at the time, but now I feel more confident every day that he's right. I don't know exactly how it works, but it's a lot like what you did in your talk with Hoke. You admit to the authority that you're in the wrong. And the ultimate authority is God himself. And he takes care of the problem for you. Since I did that, something down deep inside me tells me everything will be okay."

"Ye ain't plugged two fellers, neither, is ye?"

"Well, no, but still I haven't been perfect. I've got more warts than a

180

toadfrog, if you're looking for imperfections. And perfection is God's standard. Why, I can't so much as look at Trixie Wills without having evil thoughts. I'm glad she's married to Red Roper now and both of them are out of school. But there's lots of other girls around to look at, and a lot of the time I can't help but feel like I'm lusting or something."

"Aw, 'at's jes' natchel, son. Ain't nothin' wrong wi' 'at kind o' sinnin'. 'Ey wouldn' be many folks in th' world wi'out 'at sort o' attraction. But shootin' and killin' an' makin' hard likker—now I ain't s' sho' God's gon' be easy on 'at kind o' carryin' on. An' y' know whut, boy? I don't mean no offense, butye's startin' t' sound like 'at preacher whut lives 'crost th' road fum yo' house." Hank coughed a little as he finished the words, and his breath seemed short, coming in wheezing bursts.

"Well, the preacher from Atlanta said pretty much the same thing Mr. Holiday says. You recognize your need, that you can't make it right on your own. Then you just pray and ask Jesus into your heart, and he comes in. That's when forgiveness happens."

"I ain't s' sho' it's all 'at easy, boy. I got a heap o' studdin' t' do 'bout 'at."

"Let's just pray and ask him to come into your heart, Mr. McCard," said Travis. Beads of nervous sweat formed and his palms became sticky as he tried to communicate sincerely on such an uncommonly deep level. His mother had him pray regularly at the dinner table now, but this was different and somehow intimidating. Something urged him onward, and he sensed an unaccustomed degree of confidence surging through him. He gulped and took the plunge, and continued, "I'll pray if you'll let me."

"Hm-pf," was Hank's only response. The boy bowed his head, closed his eyes, and prayed an exceedingly simple prayer, finishing it in thirty seconds or less. He asked God to forgive Hank for killing that revenue officer so long ago, and for any other sins he might have committed. He looked up quickly as he finished, but he couldn't tell if Hank had so much as bowed his head. The old man said nothing at all, in fact. He just reached for his handkerchief and wiped away another droplet of liquid that had formed on the end of his nose.

Travis tried to continue their conversation for another half hour as twilight fell, but there were long intervals without words. Finally he said a weak goodbye, and headed back down the road home. Hank kept on rocking in silence, except for the rhythmic squeak of wooden rockers on worn porch planks. The boy looked back thoughtfully, and his old friend raised one hand just a bit in acknowledgement. He couldn't help but notice that Hank looked very frail and weak, so much so that he was amazed the old fellow had been able to walk all the way to the river just a couple of weeks before.

The boy passed the house of Homer Holiday, and noticed that the living room lights were already on. The Holidays were so frugal that they seldom used electricity when it wasn't absolutely necessary, and it was barely getting dark. He could see Homer's outline, silhouetted against the window, apparently reading. The front door was standing open, and Homer was shouting loudly and enthusiastically from time to time, "Amen, amen." There was then a period of silence, and the words were repeated with equal zeal. He wasn't surprised at such activity, which was sometimes even more animated. It was just a tad unusual that it was going on so late in the day, but he didn't think much more about it. He shrugged his shoulders and walked on down the knoll to his house.

CHAPTER 17

Travis was up fairly early the next morning, preparing to go see where the blackberries were blooming best, and maybe shoot a little with his .22 rifle. He planned to come back by Hank's place and discuss some more with him. He worried a little about what the old man thought of their brief conversation and his feeble attempt at prayer the evening before, and whether it might negatively affect their friendship. He was just pulling on his brogands when the phone rang. His mother was already up, and he heard her answer it at the telephone table in the hallway.

"Oh, hi, Gracie. How are you? He did? Oh, no! Uh-huh. Oh, my goodness, I'm so sorry. Yes, I'll tell him. Yes. Let us know if there's anything in the world we can do."

Travis heard the harsh thump of the phone as his mother hung up, and he dashed through the door with his shoelaces still untied and his shirt unbuttoned. The look in his mother's eyes was one of dread, and she looked him in the eye only for a flash, and then she turned her gaze toward the floor.

"What did Gracie say, Mama? What did she say?"

"Mr. McCard is dead," she said with resignation as she slumped toward a stiff wooden chair next to the phone. "I'm sorry, son. He died on the front porch sometime last evening. He was still in his rocking chair this morning, according to Gracie."

As she spoke, she could see her boy's eyes filling with tears, and he covered his face with his hands and retreated to the bedroom without a word. He plunged face first onto the bed and cried quietly for several minutes. His mother came in and sat on the edge of the bed, stroking his back and trying very hard to say soothing words. After a long while, he rolled over, sat up on the edge of the bed, and looked downward while he spoke.

"Mama, I was the last person to see him alive. I was there last night," he sobbed softly. "Why did he have to die?"

"Old age, I guess, son. They don't know. He's been declining in health ever since Mrs. Maggie died, you know."

"Yes, I know, Mama," said Travis through his tears. "He'd got to where he couldn't walk very far anymore without suffering. And I can't believe that I just talked to him on that porch last night. I never thought it would be the last time I'd see him alive."

"Everybody has to die sometime, son. And we're all going to miss him. What did you and Mr. McCard talk about last evening?"

"Lots of things. Mostly about Jesus and heaven and who'll be going there and who won't. He didn't seem to get the main point, though. He hardly spoke after I started talking about Jesus. I was going to go back this evening and see him again."

"You did right, son. You can't force anybody. I'm proud of you."

Ruth left the boy alone, and as she departed the room she could see a sleek black hearse from Childress Funeral Home slowly heading up the dirt road, carefully skirting hazardous deep ruts, on the way to the McCard house to retrieve the body. There was a thin early morning mist hanging over the road, and a feathery haze streamed off the sides of the hearse in most eerie fashion.

The family had discovered the old man already cold, stiff with rigor mortis, yet still rocking with his leg crossed as usual. Ruth watched with some trepidation as the dark vehicle disappeared from view, and she worried deeply about Travis, wondering what kind of effect this loss might have on him. She didn't often resent her husband's necessary absences, but right now she wished fervently for him to be home. Som of her fears were eased when the boy emerged from the bedroom with his face much more resigned and at ease, and walked into the kitchen. He began rummaging in the pantry seeking some cereal for breakfast, initially saying nothing. He got a bowl out of the cabinet, and then turned to his mother.

"Mama, we never did try to get Mr. McCard that cur dog," he said slowly, thoughtfully, as he filled his bowl with cereal. He then went to the refrigerator looking unsuccessfully for a bottle of milk, which he hadn't noticed was already out on the table. "Oh, here it is. And you know what bothers me more than anything? I haven't the faintest idea if he went to heaven."

"Let's pray that he did, son. And I don't think he'll need a cur dog there. Mrs. Maggie will be there, you know. And he'll have everything he needs."

"I know he'd be glad to see Mrs. Maggie, Mom. He thought an awful lot of her. But I don't think he'd really like it in heaven if he didn't have a cur dog," said the boy as he sat down at the table, shaking his head slowly. He poked with a spoon at the bowl of cereal, mixing it, as was his custom.

"Let's give thanks for the food, and pray for the McCards, too," said his mother.

They both bowed their heads, and Ruth prayed. She found it a little awkward to ask for it after the fact, but she went ahead anyway and petitioned specifically that perhaps the gruff old man might have made it into God's presence. Travis once more had a peculiarly intense sense that someone else was there while his mother prayed, and he even opened his eyes and looked around briefly. Bobby and Sue were still not up, and there was no one else visible.

Since the McCards had no pastor or church, they had to scramble a bit to find someone to preach the funeral. With no small amount of misgiving, they settled on Homer Holiday to officiate. The two men had very little in common, but Homer had been acquainted with Hank for many years. Hank had always expressed a great deal of worldly but honest disdain for the preacher, a fact that he had never tried to hide. Gracie was a little nervous about approaching him to do the job in the first place, but she was pleasantly surprised when the old preacher accepted the assignment with obvious elation. Homer was so eager to preach the funeral that it made Gracie quite anxious, and she took pains to make it clear to him that his remarks should be limited and brief. All the family really wanted was for someone to say a few words of comfort over their father, and not prolong it into a sermon or an ordeal. Homer agreed to abide by their wishes.

The casket was made of beautiful, polished walnut, and it gleamed with a high sheen as Hank McCard lay a corpse in his living room. It was a most peculiar sensation for Travis to gaze at the lifeless body of his old friend, and to realize that they would never again be crossing the burn to hunt squirrels. The funeral home had done a marvelous job of making him look like he was only sleeping, and he had an expression that was as content as if he had just come in from a successful hunt. He did look odd in a coat and tie, though, dressed as Travis had never seen him in life. The boy was filled with a nagging regret that talking with his old friend that last evening hadn't been more positive and reassuring.

A small country Baptist church out on the Cherokee City Road agreed to let the family use its sanctuary for the service. Flowers overflowed out the door, there were so many wreaths and sprays and simple bouquets. There was practically nobody in Indian Park who didn't know Hank McCard, and it seemed that almost all of them sent flowers. A large percentage of the town seemed to be at the funeral, too, making it a much larger affair than anyone had expected.

Homer Holiday was attired in his Sunday best for the occasion, wearing a suit that was quite dingy and old, and obviously fit a bit too tight in the middle. He had on a tie that didn't match, and freshly-polished clod-buster brogans were on his feet. Travis wondered if

Gracie had made the right choice, giving the podium to a man who had the stamina to pray all night, and who had been thrown out of practically every church in the eastern half of Cherokee County. This could be one long funeral, a guilt-ridden thought that the boy suppressed. He stoically made up his mind to endure whatever was coming.

The church organist played several old hymns, none of which the boy could recognize. It all sounded so sad and hopeless. He joined the throng that filed by the open coffin, and tried vainly to suppress another tear as he gazed at his lifeless friend one last time. The funeral home attendants then came forward, rearranged the flowers some, and closed the door on the remains of Hank McCard. It was time for Homer's final remarks, and he strode stiffly to the podium.

"Family an' friends o' Hank McCard," began the preacher in a crackling voice, his thinning hair shining in the light from some kind of tonic. "I been a mite down lately wi' lumbago, an' I got a rizen on m' neck, too, 'at 'is tie don't he'p none. An wi' 'is cancer on m' lip a-eatin' away, I ain't got much spunk lef' t' flang at ye. But I'm gon' try harder'n a blind 'possum in a 'simmon tree t' say whut th' Spirit done tol' me t' say.

"We's gathered 'ere today t' remember a life 'at touched a passel o' us in various ways. Now I don't b'lieve in preachin' nobody in, ner preachin' nobody out'n neither Heaven ner Hell, so 'ere's th' straight o' it. I might nigh couldn't o' stood up 'ere if'n ol' Hank McCard had passed away three days ago. But 'e passed away jes' two days ago, an' I got some news t' pass on t' y'all.

"I wuz studdin' m' Bible th' day befo' yestiddy, an' I jes' kep' on a-studdin'right into th' night, cause I felt th' presence o' th' Spirit like I ain't felt in many a year. I might nigh went t' shoutin', right 'ere in m' house, an' I would o' if'n I wuzn't skeered I'd agger-frit m' neighbors ha'f t' death. I helt m'se'f back some an' studded 'bout 'is revelation I wuz gittin', an' I couldn' make much sense out'n it. I fin'ly went on t' bed, still studdin'. I laid 'ere th' longest time befo' I fin'ly went t' sleep, sich sleep as it wuz.

"I dreamt a mos' peculiar dream, one whut seemed might nigh real. A star as bright as th' sun fell out'n th' sky an' landed smack in th' middle o' th' dirt road front o' m' house. It went t' shimmerin' and shakin' like th' tail on a ol' rattler, all th' while glowin' like noontime. It started shapin' up, an' fine'ly I could see 'is shiny robe. A mos' peculiar sight it wuz, an' somebody wuz wearin' 'at robe, an' turnin' to an' fro like somebody tryin' t' show it off. It wuz s' bright I couldn't hardly look at it, but b' shieldin' m' eyes I could see 'at it wuz a man o' some sort. An settin' at 'is feet wuz a right curious critter, looked fer all th' world like a old-fashioned cur dog, like I ain't seed in many a year. Th' Lawd fin'ly let me see who it wuz a-wearin' 'at robe, an' it wuz a s'prise o' all s'prises t' me. Ol' Hank McCard, 'ere, it wuz, sho' as I'm standin' 'ere, an' 'e wuz a-wearin' a robe o' righteousness, o' all thangs. It had t' be 'im, sho' 'nuff, 'at ol' hook nose ain't no mistake 'bout. 'E waved t' me, an' 'en wawked right on off out'n m' sight, wi' 'at cur dog follerin' along b'hin' 'im, lookin' happy as a dead pig in th' sunshine. An' can ye 'magine th' shock o' findin' out th' next mornin' 'at 'e done passed on?

"An' 'at's th' troof o' it, folks, sho' as m' name's Holiday. Whut else kin I say? Wuz he a good man? Did 'e he'p 'is neighbors? 'E wuz, in 'is own way, an' 'e did, when 'e could, but I ne'er thought 'e'd git 'at robe o' righteousness. But I stand 'ere convinced as a doubtin' Thomas 'at 'e's in heaven right now. An' ye kin go, too, if'n ye ax Jesus into yo' heart. I don't rightly know when ner whur Hank McCard did 'at, but ye kin bet yo' turnip crop 'e did sometime er other. An' 'ey ain't nothin' much else t' say. God bless y'all! Halelujah!"

Travis sat stunned as the whole assembly filed out. Finally his mother took him by the hand, and he walked with his family to their car. It was just a short drive to the selected gravesite, and the boy rode silently, caught up in deep thought. He said nothing, not a word, as the casket was lowered into the ground, protected with a thick concrete vault, and then covered with earth. He still hadn't spoken when he got back into the car with his mother and siblings for the trip back to Indian

Park.

"Mama," he finally said, slowly and with deliberation. "I think I wouldn't mind growing up to be a preacher. But right now I want something else."

"What's that, son?"

"A cur dog. A genuine, old-fashioned cur dog. Can we start looking right away?"

"I don't see why not, son."

"And I'm going to name him Hank."

The boy settled back into the seat and watched the green mountains flow past as they rode, wondering what life would be like without his friend. Through the sadness of their separation, though, a deep satisfaction filled his mind.

And a sustaining sense of the Presence guarded his young heart once again.

Printed in the United States
137683LV00001B/9/A